THE TYPHOON SANCTION

WES DEMOTT

Admiral House Publishing

This 2012 paperback version of THE TYPHOON SANCTION is the first printed edition.

Cover Art Credit: Walter G. Arce/shutterstock.com

For permission or further contact, email the publisher at:
RightsandPermissions@AdmiralHousePublishing.com

ISBN 978-09851741-1-8

To Sabine

Wes DeMott

1

The smog that so often shrouded Tiananmen Square was gone, carried off by the breeze that cooled the thousands of Beijing residents playing checkers or practicing tai chi on the large expanse of concrete. Hundreds more – mostly Chinese tourists – cued up for busses to The Great Wall or nearby silk market, while others stared silently at the entrance to the Forbidden City, intimidated perhaps by legend and reluctant to go in, as if the labyrinth of rooms beyond the gates were still and forever off-limits.

Alone on the steps to Mao's mausoleum, a CIA field officer, code-named Cruiser, tapped numbers into a cell phone while a signal-scrambler, piggybacked to the battery, changed encryption code two times every minute.

"Operations," came an already flat voice, further deadened and delayed by distance and unscrambling.

"Stand by," Cruiser said as two Chinese men in black pants and white shirts, one with a scar over his left eye, dashed up the steps toward him. But they passed just as quickly, the one with the scar enthusiastically recalling the bloody protest of 1989, the million students who'd swarmed the square, and the one man with a briefcase who'd heroically stopped a line of tanks.

"Deputy Director of Operations," Cruiser said, once the men were out of range and he was safe – although *safe* could only be defined tenuously and with a fine sense of relativity. Sometimes it meant nothing more than a tiny pile of rubble that deflected an enemy's fire. But more often, at least for Cruiser, *safe* was a result of being ordinary and unnoticeable as he moved efficiently through the misdirection and espionage of his world, a world recently overrun by military firepower and overt cowboy antics. Cruiser would be one of the last field officers to spend his entire career overseas under non-official cover, and he knew it.

"What have you got?" asked Nick, a man of fine details and important specifics who was ideally suited to sit behind a desk. He had no strength or training to be threatening anywhere else, but his mind and his powerful title enabled him to orchestrate world events to whatever best suited America.

"It's Sarin gas."

"How much?"

Cruiser waited on the code change, using the time to compare this assignment to dozens of others, looking for similarities or mistakes or anything useful until *Run into the jungle! I'm trying to help you* pounded in his ears and his mind jammed.

"How much?" Nick repeated.

Cruiser pushed away that long ago tragedy. "A thousand liters. Equivalent to three hundred chemical warheads."

"Jesus. Your earlier report mentioned VX gas."

Twelve more seconds for the change. Seven. Two. "That too, but less quantity. Works a lot faster though."

"Phun's ship is Liberian registry?"

"Yes."

He waited for the next code change, making a last mental run-up of the actions he was setting in motion. Nick would immediately brief the Director of Central Intelligence on the plan. The DCIA would, as usual, bypass the National Intelligence Director and go straight to the White House and brief the President. The President would, in all likelihood, approve it.

If the President didn't approve it, the CIA would build a somewhat thicker layer of deniability and execute it anyway, secretly pressuring a foreign navy to sink Phun's freighter as it crossed the Pacific, or cutting it in two with one of their own freighters, sinking both ships if necessary. Anything to keep Phun's floating bomb from making port in Norfolk.

"Phun bought the ship with his father's money," Cruiser said. "He got the toxins off the missiles Russia destroyed under treaty with us."

"That son of a bitch killed his old man for that money. What kind of an animal is this guy?"

"A rabid one."

"Shipping out of what port?"

"Vladivostok. Phun didn't want to move that stuff across the border."

Eight seconds until the code changed. Cruiser looked around. One of the two men on the steps snapped a photo of the other, and then they laughed as they walked back down to the square.

"It's a single hull ship with five tons of explosives spread throughout the hold, just above the water line. The

7

explosion will propel the gas into the air, and depending on the wind he expects to contaminate all warships at the Naval Operations Base and kill a million or so people in Hampton Roads."

"Okay, Cruiser, it's about a twenty day ocean crossing. We'll intercept the ship. You take care of Phun. He's been a nuisance before, but now I'm sanctioning him."

"I understand. No problem."

"Killing Phun? You can't be serious."

"Of course it's a problem. But I'll handle it."

"Lots of unfortunate things happen at sea that can never be explained. I'll see that his sunken ship is one of them. Let me know when you're completed."

"Roger that. Good luck with the intercept. I'd hate to see America dirty-bombed."

Cruiser hung up and walked toward home, surprised he'd just used such a useless word as hate. Words like fear, shame, and terror, most often shrouded or sanitized by much nobler words like courage, necessity, and expedience, all fit neatly into the puzzle of his life, but hate was awkward because he had carried his for so long and unknowingly. The only way that could have happened was by his refusal to face it, which meant he'd allowed something so ugly to fester inside him, dormant and waiting.

As he walked toward home he tried, as always, to see his surroundings as others might. More tourists were arriving at the square, pouring out of the subway and busses and crowding kiosks to buy souvenirs, but noticing nothing other than the obvious. A few were white and round eyed, searching constantly for anyone with whom they could communicate in English, yet instinctively suspicious of the dozens of choppy translators offering to serve as tour guides.

Soldiers stood ceremoniously on guard, keying on the attention they received more than the possibility of an attack. Their job was to serve as a deterrent by being an obvious threat, whereas the career Cruiser had chosen required that his actions were never obvious, and the results never carried his fingerprints.

But had he really chosen his career? If he was truly running – no, he *was* running – his career had been nothing more than an escape *from* something that scared him rather than *to* something he wanted.

It took ten minutes to get to his safe house, which was nothing of the sort. Down a tight alley and through a door with broken hinges, the small, dirty room was not even part of a house, nor was it anything close to safe. Rather it was a small old office building that had long ago worn out and then served as a whorehouse until its derelict appearance scared off the patrons. Ever since the girls left and the illegal bar closed, the rooms had been let on a daily and cash only basis.

But it was perfect for Cruiser because he had nothing to hide that he didn't carry around at all times, and the safety and comfort he sacrificed was more than offset by his invisibility. People disappeared into places like that and no one ever cared or came looking for them.

He'd seen enough of the CIA's new breed to know they would never settle for anywhere so perfect, trying instead to stay unnoticed in hotels with familiar names, maids who searched everything, and bellmen whose primary source of income was information. It was a new CIA these days, one in which Cruiser had very grave doubts, but he was determined not to concern himself with its success or failure once he got out.

He changed into clean but worn-out clothing before going to work at the vendor's market, all the while hoping it was actually possible to kill Phun, and trying to ignore the reality that headquarters could have assigned an entire team of elite operators to kill him, and even they couldn't guarantee success against someone invisible.

Although he trusted Nick and usually gave Langley the benefit of the doubt, Cruiser had seen enough in his career to wonder if someone had already devised a plan to win regardless of whether it was he or Phun who died. After all, Cruiser knew a career's worth of lies that had moved men to upper floors with windowed offices, as well as the truths that could send them back down again, or worse. As sweaty nights continued to spin into new and dangerous days, Cruiser understood how the Assistant Directors would also hate his ownership of the facts behind their ascensions. That kept him watching his back, although there was nothing new about that.

But there were other things that were new, and this mission was one of them. Before the attacks of 9/11, headquarters would never have sanctioned an individual like Phun, because for all of Phun's well earned reputation for cruelty and stealth he was really nothing more than a rich and powerful brat lining up to take his shot at America. He wouldn't normally have justified the political risks or international fallout involved in assassination, but the U.S.G. had been sanctioning high-threat loonies like Phun more and more often because ignoring them was just too risky.

From the beginning, Cruiser knew that Operation Typhoon – some analyst's careless play on Phun's name –

would challenge the best of his abilities by pitting him against his toughest target ever. Phun was not only a savage, he was at least as much a ghost as Cruiser. No verifiable photos of Phun existed anywhere in the media or Chinese archives, and no one was able or willing to give a description. The only thing Cruiser knew at the start was that Phun was an outstanding warrior who loved nothing more than to stain his hands with the blood of his victims. Phun disseminated that information widely and with proud delight, like a threat to all potential challengers.

It had taken months just to learn that Phun had a wife and kids, and where they all lived. So for the three months since, Cruiser had risen each morning in his tiny room, cleaned himself as best he could in the stained sink down the hall, and then hobbled uneasily to the market on Phun's street, where he posed as a crippled vendor, hot in his makeup and disguise, his legs cramping as he kneeled on a woven mat and chanted his sales pitch in Mandarin.

But even with his finely honed ability to alter his appearance, he could never look Chinese. So as he'd done so often in so many other countries, he'd created a mixed-breed disguise that served him well enough. His mother could have been Chinese and slept with an American businessman in Hong Kong or a Merchant Marine in Shenzhen. Perhaps she'd been a Caucasian who'd slept with a traveling Chinese athlete or entertainer. It really didn't matter what people thought when they saw him, just as long as it kept him from drawing attention. Kept him invisible in plain sight. Vanilla.

Week after week he'd blended just barely into the homogenous covey of retailers who hawked fake Rolexes and knock-off Timberlands from wooden carts and tiny storefronts, and Cruiser worked just as hard to sell his black market DVDs – a product he'd chosen specifically because the growing crackdown on intellectual property rights would prove him a criminal if he ever needed to convince one of Phun's men.

Within a week, the other vendors accepted him fully as a handicapped product of miscegenation who wasn't selling much from his mat, and so whenever they ate a meal they traded their best scraps and meatiest castoffs for whatever movie was least likely to sell, trying to help him survive without offending him. Cruiser lived on those scraps so he would not only look but smell like the peasant he pretended to be.

But he never saw anyone he thought might be Phun or a member of his family, even with near-constant surveillance on the fortressed home across the street. All he'd managed to do was secretly click photos of the men who visited.

His only break came a few weeks back when the local police arrested one of Phun's men for murdering an American businessman. Cruiser immediately called Nick, who once again did the impossible, and in less than an hour the man was free to go, or at least would be once Cruiser had his chance to interrogate the doomed soul.

Under Nick's specific instructions, two uniformed police officers marched the man ceremoniously down the street in full view of a very curious public. They opened the door to the empty office Cruiser had found on short notice and pushed the man inside. Then they left.

"Have a seat," Cruiser said in Chinese from the deepest shadows of the darkened room. "Tell me what you told the police in order to get released."

"I said nothing."

"I don't believe that and Phun won't either. You know he's not one to take chances,"

"Of course not. He will kill me."

"There's nothing I can do to stop that."

The man's eyes stayed level as he clenched the fingers of his trembling hand.

"He will kill your family too."

"There is no question."

"He'll show more respect, though. Less savagery than the torture you'll endure."

"I pray he will honor them with that."

"I might be able to save them."

"I assume that's why we're talking."

"You'll need to go to Phun, as though to plead for their lives. You'll die there, of course."

"You'll save my family?"

"I will."

Cruiser put the man in play two days before calling Nick because he was sure Langley was going to authorize Phun's killing. If they hadn't, he could probably have called his asset back, but that hadn't happened and so Cruiser kneeled on his mat and waited. His legs ached, pumped full of adrenaline yet forced to stay still as his assassin went into Phun's house. If everything went better than Cruiser had any reason to hope, in a few minutes his murderer would blow himself and Phun to pieces in his study.

A young woman stopped to buy a DVD, standing directly in front of him and blocking his view of Phun's house. He glanced up and forced a quick guess as to whether or not she might be part of Phun's countermeasures, but there was nothing to support that suspicion so he gave her a smile and the DVD, rushing as though closing shop and anxious to leave. She ate up twenty seconds, perhaps a little less. His assassin couldn't have gone more than a few steps into the house.

Suddenly the bomb exploded in the wrong end of the house, somewhere near the kitchen. The huge blast shattered shop windows all along the street, blowing over vendor's carts and hurting Cruiser's ears. Everyone panicked as huge pieces of Phun's house filled the air like bombs while smaller pieces became shrapnel.

As Cruiser abandoned his handicapped pretense in order to dodge a flying piece of timber, two men stumbled out of the less-damaged shambles at the far end of Phun's house. They were coughing up dust but they had their guns out and ready to fight off whatever attack might be coming.

He'd seen both of them before and felt pretty sure that neither man was Phun, and no one else ran out of the house. So either Phun wasn't home or he'd evacuated to a bomb shelter or escape tunnel. He was definitely alive, though. The two men wielding guns would never run that risk of arrest unless Phun was still alive to save them.

Cruiser was still searching the scene when an old woman plowed into him as she ran with a bloody child in her arms. The kid was badly wounded, but if he lived there didn't appear to be any other serious casualties outside of Phun's house, and that meant Cruiser's attack was in line with his personal mandate that no one died who wasn't associated with the threat. He could have blown up the whole block to kill Phun, and perhaps that's what he should have done, but that price was too high for Cruiser, just slightly higher than failure and therefore un-payable, although it forced Cruiser to stare now into the eyes of failure for the first time in his career.

Nick would still be able to sink the freighter on the open ocean, but Phun was rich enough to buy more ships and weapons, or find even more damaging ways to attack America. He had to be killed, but Cruiser had failed to do it, and now Phun would abandon the wreckage of his home and completely disappear, becoming more of a ghost than he'd been his whole life, his already intense hatred of America amplified by the attack he would guess came from the States.

Cruiser took a last look at the men with guns and then chased after the old woman who was halfway down the next block and running in the direction of the hospital.

Three Months Later

Jay Stewart sat in his Jeep near Hatteras lighthouse, dry and comfortable on the rainy morning as he watched surfers between swipes of his windshield's wipers. Their youth gave him another dose of satisfaction that the little boy in China had lived and was perhaps even now having a similar kind of fun with his friends.

A shard of a large kitchen knife had exploded out of Phun's house and ripped through his guts, but even as the hysterical old woman stood screaming for help inside the hospital, Cruiser was calling in favors and making threats to make sure the kid got the best medical care available anywhere, every bit as good as a military general or political minister. If he hadn't, the jagged chunk of stainless steel would have killed the boy.

But that happened months ago in what was truly another life, just one more closed chapter of his *Cruiser* era that ended the moment he kept his promise to his assassin by resettling his family in Houston.

The food, language, worn clothes and dirty rooms were all dark memories on which Cruiser had thrown the switch and turned out the light. It was finally time for him to be Jay Stewart, remembering, if possible, how to be a peaceful man who thought innocently of those around him, stopped worrying about drawing suspicion, and moved without expecting attack – all things about which he'd fantasized since his murderous romp through the jungle.

There were a few challenges ahead before he could get there, and they kept him from joining the surfers as the heavy rain that battered their faces – the last rain the Carolina coast would get before the approaching hurricane hit – glassed over the six-foot waves that broke in clean lefts. His first purchase after settling in Buxton, even before buying his home, had been a new surfboard that he'd carefully leaned into the corner of his motel room, and took out surfing a few times. He wanted to go home and get it now, but he still had too much to do as he learned his new career as a realtor. So he'd exiled himself from the water.

When he'd turned fifty a month ago, surfing – finding the emotional balance to be in harmony with nature – once again became a top priority. Ride waves for a couple of hours in the morning and then go for breakfast and talk about different breaks with young surfers who would accept him without really knowing him, the way surfers always did if no territorial issues were at stake.

But in reality, they did know him, or at least knew *of* him. Since he'd moved back from China he'd heard the story several times, and seen his picture in every souvenir store and tourist trap on the island.

"True photo," the surf shop owner told a wide-eyed kid who interrupted the conversation he and Stewart were having about sales figures and inventory. "Not one of those computer enhancements."

"Outrageous," said the young surfer as his buddy bragged about having the same picture hanging in his bedroom.

"That was one hell of a hurricane," the shop owner said. "Destroyed the coast, flooded the eastern seaboard, and sank tankers with sixty-foot waves. Yet that guy paddled out. He was the only one who dared it."

Stewart glanced at the photo of him in a full banzai stance, feet wide apart and arms stretched out, screaming down the face of the biggest wave he'd ever seen anywhere, including magazines. Both the weather and the wave were dark and ominous like they were out to kill him, nature in a bad mood and refusing to be tamed, while his white board looked like an angel or ghost, an ethereal specter in the raging clutches of disaster.

"Naah, it's gotta be fake," said the kid. "How could he even paddle out in that mess?"

"I was there," the storeowner lied. "Nothing fake about it. Just a gutsy guy going way over line."

"Wow," said Stewart, just to make them look at him as a test of recognition, something he'd done thousands of times as Cruiser, and usually with the same empty result. "Crazy bastard."

The kids turned back to the photo without giving Stewart another thought, and although that satisfied him it also showed how powerfully his past still ruled his present. He'd always loved doing dangerous things for which he was recognized by the smallest number of people – none, if at all possible – but he needed to accept being recognized if he ever wanted to have friends in his new life.

As he waited for the kids to leave, he doubted he could ever change. It seemed rooted too deeply, one of his few character traits that was original issue and not a product of training. He'd been secretive since his youth, and so the Agency had nothing to do with it beyond their skillful manipulation.

17

But who knew for sure in a situation like his, when after twenty-five years of service to America the amorphous Cruiser, who existed only in shadows and rumor, was about to disappear altogether?

It was Nick – his boss at Langley – who first suggested retirement when Cruiser returned from Beijing.

"You really want people shooting at you when you're fifty-five or sixty?"

"I didn't really fail in China, if that's what you mean. I did manage to divert Phun's attention from war with America, Nick."

"Sure. Now his only interest is killing you, the guy who murdered his family."

"Certainly makes him predictable and lowers his threat level."

"It also creates a problem that highlights the advantage of retiring. God knows how easily you could slip into obscurity in that little Carolina town you love so much."

His cell phone rang and a woman with an English accent said, "Hello, Mr. Stewart?"

As he sat in his Jeep he fought the instinct to stay silent, or to confirm her identity or clearance, trying to imagine what kind of a person he might have been if his life hadn't been derailed by that first sight of a life draining through two bullet holes in a man's head.

"Yes," he answered, but despite his hope to sound engaging it still had that flat, give-away-nothing monotone he'd spent decades perfecting.

"Uh…bad time? Did I catch you at a bad time?"

He tried again. "Sorry. Yes, this is Jay Stewart with Hatteras Realty."

He almost laughed about how pissed off his dead enemies would be to know the ultra-professional government agent who'd killed them was now hawking sand and lumber and summer rentals for something to do just to stay busy.

"It's Jennifer. About the house on the sound. I met some nice people in town and lost track of time and now I'm running late. Terribly bad manners, I know."

"No problem. I've got another contract to write so the extra time actually works out for me. How about three?"

"Perfect. So nice of you to be flexible."

"Glad to help."

As he hung up he wondered if she'd really met people in town. She had an interesting reputation in the dark and secretive world in which they worked as an extremely smart woman who could accomplish a great deal while appearing to waste time, and he'd just given her two more hours to do it.

He wasn't really worried about what she might do with the time, but he was a little disappointed with the delay because he'd lied about writing a contract and this was his first property showing. He was anxious to know if real estate might be satisfying in the next phase of his life because he sure wasn't doing it for the money. Decades of traveling on a government account, unable even to get his paychecks, had piled up more cash than he would ever need. In his future life he would just need something to do.

He left the beach and pulled onto the road, wondering if Phun already knew where he was, and too well aware of how Phun intended to kill him. It was scary to have Phun hunting him, but Stewart had better local knowledge and that gave him the advantage. Countless surgeries since the plane crash had changed his face so much that even if an old photo of him existed it would useless. And though he was still strong, it was now in a lean and stringy way, powered by the mental toughness of a life lived hard. He had tinted contacts, a neat beard, and short dyed hair that made him look entirely different from the muscular longhaired surfer anyone might have known or photographed so long ago.

And he was average, of course, in height and weight, while his other physical features were subject to so much change that his personnel record read like a cast of unrelated characters. Professionally, there were rumors that Cruiser was black, and others that he was an Arab. Some thought Cruiser might be a woman, or not even exist at all.

The most popular legend was that he actually *had* died in Africa, and that headquarters had assigned Cruiser's codename to several other field officers as a way to enhance the image of their capabilities. America's enemies loved that theory, finding comfort in the belief that his devastating work was the result of many, and not just one dangerously invisible hunter.

But now, for the first time, Stewart was the hunted. He set up the game as he always had, though, by pitting his craftiness against the power and courage of his enemy. If he did an exceptional job he would survive and finally kill Phun, bringing that assignment in line with CIA expectations.

Regardless of whether he won or lost, Stewart was making complex plans that would, no doubt, give the locals something else to talk about. Just as he'd done by paddling out during the hurricane, he was going to attempt another deadly feat and then hide completely from the recognition. He was pretty sure that when the time came and the blood spilled, he could protect the innocent locals from becoming collateral damage.

He got to the house for sale just as a Ford Expedition pulled into the drive and parked between stilts that elevated the home for when storms sent seawater sweeping from ocean to sound.

"Jesus Christ," popped out of his mouth as a woman in her mid thirties hopped out of the car. "You *never* considered she'd look like this."

Jennifer was short and petite, about five foot three in white sneakers and barely over a hundred pounds. She had straight brown hair, tied in a ponytail, and dark brown eyes set off by sharp Anglican features.

She gazed briefly across the backyard at Pamlico Sound, then turned and walked up the driveway as Stewart cursed himself for being so stupid for so long about something so familiar. Looking different from people's expectations was his favorite trick, and yet now he was the victim. For more than a year he'd made dozens of important assumptions about this woman and her family based on logical expectations, and he'd relied heavily upon them. And all that time he'd been wrong.

"I'm Jay Stewart."

"Jennifer. Nice to finally meet you. Sorry again for being late." She smiled as she reached out her hand, and as she did he checked her for false or positive signals, anything that might provide good insight into her. He was even more focused since he'd already been wrong once about her.

She was pretty, engaging, and very much aware of the power she held in lowering her head a little and looking into a man's eyes a half-second longer than she should, and although Stewart was fascinated by women who did this well, he never fell for it. He expected Jennifer to do it if she thought he could help her, but he also suspected she was

21

discriminating in her use of it. He didn't figure her as the type of woman who charmed every man she met out of habit or instinct, but that jury was still out.

There was something more about her, a veiled intensity – either intelligence or instinct or both – that operated fluidly behind the girlishness she used to disguise her brutality. Everyone had a persona that worked in most arenas, and Jennifer's clearly exploited her looks. But it wasn't her, at least not the real her. He'd read the reports and seen photos of her carnage, but there was much more to learn about her and it intrigued him.

"Nice vehicle."

"I borrowed it from a friend I'm staying with in Manteo. Really nice guy. It's got a permit for driving on the beach so I've been doing that a lot. It's fun."

"You're staying with a man in Manteo?" He watched closely, but the personal nature of the question didn't shock her at all.

She covered her mouth as though she'd let out a secret. "You won't tell my parents will you? You live here, I suppose. Do you spend every night alone?"

She was drawing him in skillfully, using the tools of human nature to make herself seem familiar. Then, strategically, she pulled back her hand, denying and teasing him, hammering playfully at the hard barrier that separated his human emotions from his professional instincts. She hadn't gazed up or cocked her head but he could feel her putting him at ease. She was good, no doubt about it.

"So…this is the house," she said as she looked up at the two-story home on stilts with a wraparound porch. She stared, but didn't really seem to see the house or the grounds or the view. She either had another agenda or was anxious to get somewhere else, although most people probably wouldn't have noticed because the clues were too subtle.

"Yes, this is the house."

"Is it just me or is it a little hard on the eyes?"

"It's supposed to look like a home in the Caribbean, I think. The bright colors could be repainted."

"Then I'd probably do that. Definitely."

"Want to look inside?"

"Can't imagine passing up the chance."

He walked up and unlocked the door, pushed it open, and went in. She didn't follow, so he stood there dealing with the big flock of butterflies he'd had since first seeing her. They weren't the kind he got in combat or when he was trapped, and they fell very short of the kind he had when he'd been tortured. But against his better judgment and every single one of his defenses, he liked her right off, just the way he was sure she'd expected long ago when she'd decided to use him for introductions around town. He knew his feelings were obvious to her. Worse yet, he couldn't really make himself care anymore.

He'd liked plenty of women before but his job had never allowed him the distraction, so maybe this uncomfortable new feeling had less to do with Jennifer and more with his new emotional latitude to feel anything at all.

She saw how awkward he was and couldn't seem to resist making it worse by staring hard as he fumbled around in the doorway. She crossed her arms over her stomach, tilted her head, and smiled as if refusing to speak or follow until he in some small way acknowledged her impact on him.

He turned away, giving her the smallest hint that he was better prepared for the game they'd just begun because he knew what she didn't, that one day soon she'd discover how desperately she needed him.

It was good to have superior knowledge like that.

She took a step back and turned around. "Afraid I don't like the house at all. Think I really want to be over there on the beach side."

"I don't blame you."

"Any chance you'd like to get an early dinner with me? My treat."

"No thanks."

"Oh?"

Now she was the one to look surprised, as if no one had ever turned her down before. Which was probably the truth.

"See…well, I kind of wanted to talk to you about the town. What it's like to live here, what the people do, things like that. Thought we could do it over a meal."

"Sorry, I ate a late lunch." He waited until he saw more confusion over how to deal with him. "But all right. I guess I could eat something. What kind of food do you like?"

"It's not really that important to me. I don't want to put you out."

"I do have a lot of work I need to get finished."

"How about I follow you to somewhere casual, Mr. Stewart?"

She waited for him to say "Jay" but he wouldn't do it.

"Sounds fine."

They went to their cars, and as he pulled onto the road a truck crossed the centerline and nearly hit him, snapping him out of the game he was playing and reminding him that he could never afford to drop his guard against Phun, not even in this brand new life as Jay Stewart.

2

Stewart led the pretty woman with the skillful smile down a narrow rural road to a dockside fish house. He'd won their first engagement but just barely, the initial setback of her appearance throwing him off pretty badly. Reactions always needed to be carefully measured, even in the face of a colossal mistake like that, but he'd been so surprised that his had shown a little.

He'd compensated by squirming in her presence as he stood in the doorway, acting as though it was her beauty, and not her non-Asian looks, that made him feel awkward. A stammering man had to make her feel empowered, which would logically lead her to relax.

Even if he had been sincere, it didn't matter, because even assuming her flirting had in any way been genuine, deception had already doomed whatever small or great friendship they might have the potential of sharing. Their entire encounter earlier had been based on a long and intricate string of lies dating back almost a year, perpetrated independently between them both and culminating in her coming to Buxton under the pretense of looking for a home – which was merely her cover as she tried to track down Cruiser to get the most recent details of the mission on which she was embarking. Once she had that information she would move on to China and never think back on the people she'd met, especially the ones she might have liked, even a little. It was the only way for people like them to work professionally.

Besides, if she'd wanted to be his ally or friend she could have easily set the stage with honesty by going through channels and asking for the meeting. But her reputation had convinced Stewart that she counted herself too smart, efficient, and confident – or perhaps just too insecure – to ask for help. In every previous operation in which she'd had a significant role she'd always chosen the most dangerous ground and difficult procedures as if they were necessary to prove and re-prove her merits and abilities, if only to herself, hiding any possible vulnerability behind an impenetrable image of confidence.

Early on in his career, Stewart had been the same way. But as he'd matured he learned that weakness was something to feign often, and that relying on strength in the covert world was a liability far more often than it could ever be an asset.

Her reasons for wanting to use Cruiser were certainly clear enough, but Stewart had to consider if she had an idea that he planned to use her too, or how much blood she'd have on her hands if he succeeded. At the house she showed no suspicion that he and Cruiser might be the same person, and if that was true she couldn't have any clue to the strategy behind his fumbling real estate agent persona unless she was better than him or lucky as hell. He'd earned the right to doubt she was better, but like any true professional, he gave the usual factor to luck.

They parked next to each other and went into The Harpooner, a converted icehouse built out over the water. It was unique structurally but with the standard issue décor of most southern seafood restaurants: wooden crab traps stacked in the corners, fishing nets covering the ceiling, cork buoys hung on the walls and Old Bay flavoring the sea breeze that drifted through open windows.

They sat at a table by the windows that overlooked Buxton's small harbor. Two expensive yachts tugged on blue anchor line while thick gray lines tethered a small fleet of old fishing boats, a homemade houseboat, and a half-sunk dinghy. A fifty-foot fishing trawler, wearing its rusted rigging and faded paint as proud scars from decades of battle with the Atlantic, unloaded its catch at an adjoining dock as men in white rubber boots tossed fish onto a conveyor to the wholesaler next door, while the skipper looked on from the door of the wheelhouse.

A waitress handed out plastic menus, recited the daily specials, and suggested crab cakes. She was a plain girl about nineteen, and it occurred to Stewart that if he had a daughter she could be about the same age. He wondered what his own child might have looked like, the kind of thought he'd had often since moving back. It was strong proof that he was changing because he would have never allowed himself to consider that when traveling the world. Families were something a good spy gave up for the job because either there was never the chance to have one, or they'd had one and lost it. Both situations were dangerous to ponder.

The young guys coming up seemed to do a better job of balancing families, but of course they did their job differently too. Insertion, rendition, and extraction were words of little meaning in the way Cruiser worked, but they were battle cries for the new guys who planned their trips back home before they even went on assignment, prizing the quick in-and-out missions that offered instant stats and bragging rights but few chances at solid, human-to-human, voluntarily-given intelligence. The new breed of field officer was lousy at the long-term subtleties necessary to gather good data, but did their best to compensate by pounding the truth out of suspects. It might be the more expedient option in the ticking-bomb mentality of the day and so Cruiser never weighed in on the argument, but it was an option he would never consider.

"I'm going with the crab cakes," said Stewart, and both he and the waitress turned to Jennifer.

"Now here's the problem," she said, slapping closed the menu and then working that great smile of hers. "Whatever I order, when the meals come I bet yours is going to look better. So here's what we'll do. I'll have the fresh catch and we'll share. Deal?" Her smile turned pensive and cute.

Her boss had bragged to Nick that she could get a person so wrapped up in having fun that they dropped all their guards and spilled their guts readily. What an incredible asset in their line of work. With just a cute look and a few words about splitting a meal, she had Stewart feeling almost silly, something he hadn't allowed since he loved and then lost Simone to secrecy and travel, and then lost her to God a few years after their separation. Simone would want him to enjoy this moment with Jennifer, and although it felt unfaithful to a deep devotion, it also felt good. So he smiled suspiciously, not only to hide his feelings but also to get the questions started – questions she either would or wouldn't answer, but that would make her reveal herself either way.

"My, my, Mr. Stewart, what are you grinning at?"

"Nothing." It was one of the few truthful things he ever planned to say to her.

"You look so guilty of something."

"I probably am."

"Goes for me too, I suppose. Do you know England? Ever been there?"

"I don't like to leave America. I'm uncomfortable in strange places."

"Then perhaps I'm safe."

"From what?"

"From my naughty reputation back home." She worked her smile like an expert. "It's hard for me to imagine not traveling, though. Such an interesting world."

"I was in Mexico once. A love boat kind of vacation."

"Hardly counts. You really should go to England."

"What if I learn your reputation?"

"I suppose I could risk it."

"Was it your interest in traveling that brought you to the States?"

"I thought I'd mentioned that my family sent me here to buy a home we could all use on holiday.

"You did, that's right. You have a big family?"

"Not really. My father passed away." She looked out at the harbor as if placing her father on the deck of one of the boats at anchor. "God, he would have loved this place. It's so…I don't know. Quaint. Real. He and I shared a love of places like this. I hope to find one to call my home someday."

"Maybe here. Do people ever tell you that you have an interesting look."

She dragged her eyes away from her father and laughed as though questioning a clumsy chess move. "You just did, so now how am I supposed to take that?"

"As a good thing. Your parents weren't both English."

"Just my mum. My father was Chinese."

She put her elbows on the table and propped up her chin with her hands, staring at Stewart and waiting. Unless she had figured out who he was – and that was wildly unlikely – she was just practicing her craft while having fun with a local guy. But even in fun, with nothing apparently at stake, she was quite the expert.

"It's a pretty look for you. I mean, you're very pretty."

"Really?" She straightened a little, thrown just slightly. But then she put her chin right back in her hands as if to re-pose the way he liked. It was mostly strategy, but not completely.

"Your mother's still alive, I hope."

"I don't see her much, Mr. Stewart."

"Jay. So who else is there besides your brother?"

The dreaded direct question that so often and easily led to suspicion or attack. But he had to know if there were other threats, alliances, or accomplices that needed to be watched, so he'd had to either risk them or ask it. Now to look for truth or lies in her answer, an answer that, just like the question, would have little to do with family.

"Just him," she said, clearly suspicious of his question but seeming to have trouble coming up with a reason. "Why?"

He was ready with the covering story he expected to work. "You said your family sent you here to buy a home. I'm trying to figure out how big a house you'll need."

"Uh-uh."

The young waitress brought their food. They ate and talked, but when finished they ordered another drink instead of leaving.

"How long have you lived in Buxton?"

"I've had a place here for years."

"Then you know everyone in town, I suppose."

30

"Sure."

"My brother asked me to say hello to a guy he met when he was last here. Owned an insurance company, I think. A black man. African-American, that is, although obviously we don't use that term in the UK."

"You don't know his name?"

"No, but he always drives a Mercedes."

"You know what he does and what he drives, but not his name?"

"If you don't know him, just say so. It's not a big deal."

"I never said I didn't know him."

An excited crowd of surfers came in. One of them was regaling the others with a big-wave story, and it reminded Stewart that confessing to being the surfer in the hurricane photo would prove that he really was going in the right direction, successfully abandoning the life that denied him a family while sumptuously feeding the lie that he wasn't really running, all the while providing a steady fix of the high-octane adrenaline to which he'd long been addicted.

But not yet.

"So you know the man? Don't know him?"

Stewart pointed toward the door as a handsome black man in his late forties walked in. The hostess waved the man toward a table as if he ate all his meals there at about this time, which Stewart knew he very nearly did.

As he walked through the room he looked at Stewart the same way he always did. It wasn't a malevolent look but it wasn't friendly either; more the look of surprise and curiosity a man might give someone he'd fought and beaten but who kept getting up to fight again.

"If you buy a house here, Lenny can insure it."

The shift threw Jennifer. "What? Who?"

31

"Lenny," he said, loud enough for the man to hear. "He's the local insurance agent. The guy you asked about."

The black man changed direction and walked over. "You say something about me?"

Stewart refused to react, although he wanted to. He was moving further into his strategy to flush out Phun, and it now required Lenny's participation along with Jennifer's. He had to keep sufficient distance. Making it personal would be unprofessional and foolish, and Stewart was neither.

He smiled up at the man and then motioned for him to sit down. "I did. Care to join us?"

"You look familiar, but have we ever actually met?"

"Sure we have."

The man sat slowly but looked relieved. "Glad about that. Thought I was going nuts. Where?"

"You and I talked at breakfast a while back. Remember?"

"No, don't think that was me."

"Sure it was. You gave me some great advice about hurricane insurance for my house."

"Don't think so. But hey, maybe."

"I'm sure of it. Glad, too, now that we're predicted to take a pretty good hit from this storm heading our way."

"Okay, then I guess that's where I know you from. Thought it might be some old memory from a long time back, like maybe we went to school together or something."

"You grow up in Nebraska?"

"Got to be from breakfast then."

"Jennifer might need to talk to you." Stewart glanced over at her, and just as expected she was leaning forward and paying close attention, too excited about meeting Lenny to keep it all hidden from a person like Stewart.

"Her brother suggested she talk to you about insurance on the home I'm trying to sell her."

"I know your brother? Great."

"He's English," Stewart said. "Right, Jennifer?"

"Uh...sure, he's like me. I haven't picked the property yet, but –"

"When you do, let me know." Lenny rose to leave. "Now if you folks will excuse me."

"We were about to leave anyway," Stewart said. "Good seeing you again."

Stewart and Jennifer left and walked through the darkening parking lot toward their cars.

"Wind's picking up," he said. "Feels good."

She turned her face to the fresh breeze, closed her eyes, and smiled, natural and pretty. She stood still for several seconds, then opened her eyes and smiled again.

"Care to take a ride with me? I'll show you the hot spots around town."

She laughed lightly, as was her obligation, and then quickly became too focused on digging around in her purse for her car keys. "Let's do it tomorrow in the daylight. While I look at other homes."

"I've got a list in the office."

"Then that would be nice."

As they got to her car she closed her purse and took a step back toward the restaurant. "Bloody hell, I must have left my keys inside."

"No problem, we'll find them." He watched closely because he knew what she had to do. He wasn't playing fair, but it didn't matter because they were both playing games that weren't fair. That was the point.

"They're most likely on the table. I'll get them. Want to meet at that breakfast place you mentioned? Around nine?"

"That'll work. Guess I'll see you then." He turned and she said goodbye to his back. He got in his Jeep and drove away, catching a glimpse of Jennifer looking back at him as she returned to the restaurant. He'd seen her put her keys in her purse, but it didn't matter that she lied to him. She needed to talk to Lenny, and that was exactly what Stewart needed her to do.

* * *

Phun Xiadeng slouched in his rented Impala, parked in a far dark corner of the restaurant parking lot. Anyone could have tapped on the glass and asked what he was doing, and that made him feel exposed, but certainly not afraid. He had a good knife he'd bought as he drove up and down the island familiarizing himself with the terrain on which he would fight his enemy.

Phun had never before been to the United States, and he didn't care for what he saw. There were too many choices and too many opinions, too many people with silly careers and overweight children, too much focus on the individual and not enough interest in anything important. China was better, where thousands of years of hard work and tradition had created a respectful culture he loved and wanted to protect.

Even though Buxton was small, Phun's task would have been impossible if he hadn't managed to get a physical description of the elusive Cruiser. Up until a month ago, Phun had firmly believed the rumor that Cruiser was female, which would have denied him the chance to fully honor his family because the value of vengeance correlated to the obstacles overcome, and a woman could never give him enough of a fight. So he was glad that Cruiser turned out to be a strong and capable opponent who might provide a colossal struggle that Phun would win, but not easily, and then take back a body part to leave at his family's grave.

He had followed the black man to the restaurant, working the information that the greatest personal enemy he'd ever imagined had retired to Buxton, bought a nice Mercedes, and taken over a successful insurance business. A half-hour later, that man left the restaurant with the same attractive woman who'd walked out earlier with another man, but then returned.

He hated this black man, but even as that tore at his insides he couldn't resist watching the woman. Whatever held his attention in the dim light was stronger than mere physical attraction, as though he was bound to her in some unexplainable way. Maybe his people had passed along some information about her to help him survive. Something made him think she was dangerous. Was she a spy he'd encountered in his past, perhaps years ago? His personal bias aside, he knew there were plenty of good women spies, so it was certainly possible.

The black man laughed about something. The woman spoke over his laughter, suddenly loud enough to be heard above the wind. Phun heard her accent, British and strange in this southern town, "the world's language" his father had said.

Until arriving in America, Phun hadn't spoken a word of it in years. He preferred any dialect of Chinese, just as he preferred China's tiers of society over western democracy. There was no place for either the language or the politics of the West among a billion people where the many worked for the few. Even if democracy had succeeded in England and America – which he doubted – it would only lead

China to chaos, and that chaos would eventually cost Phun his wealth, power, and prestige.

His enemy and the woman left together in her SUV, but Phun wouldn't follow because anyone could be watching him. Cruiser must be working with a partner who was covering his back or why else would he walk along so carelessly with the woman? Or had he set this up as a trap? If Phun exposed himself now, he might step into the crosshairs of someone he wasn't anticipating.

He would kill his enemy when the man came back for his Mercedes. He couldn't imagine anyone leaving such an expensive car unattended for very long, so it was a good enough plan.

But as the taillights of the woman's car eased into the darkness, Phun started the Impala and idled out of the lot without turning
on lights. He knew he should wait exactly where he was, but something about the woman made it impossible.

* * *

After Jennifer left him to go back for her keys, Jay Stewart drove a half mile away and then parked behind a gas station at the main road. It was there that he'd turned into Cruiser once again, ready to stalk people the way he'd done for so many years in so many countries where he had so few allies.

The trick to becoming invisible was an understanding of other people and their cultures, how and when they noticed something, and why they made such predictable choices. Knowing that information allowed him to operate in public without being noticed, hiding openly in the schism between reality and people's expectation of it.

Only recently had he realized that this exceptional ability to disappear in a crowd was too isolated a way to live, especially now as he looked beyond this career to a life after. There would be no missions in that life. No targets or assignments to challenge his mind or fill his days. Sometimes – most often when bored out of his skull while waiting – he tried to get glimpses of himself in the years ahead, but the vague haze of his invisible present made it impossible.

He'd made simple changes to his look by putting on a Nike hat, black framed glasses, and a windbreaker with FDNY screened boldly on the chest: details so obvious that people would notice and remember them instead of facial details or body types.

But all the while he'd stayed out of sight, using those measures as backup precautions only, the easiest way for a witness to describe him if he were caught in the headlights of an oncoming car or a kid running through back yards plowed into him. The real trick to invisibility was not being seen in the first place.

He grabbed his backpack and trotted toward the restaurant, rushing to get there before Lenny and Jennifer left. When he got close he picked a good spot in the dark, just as the two of them walked up to her Expedition.

For an accomplished spy in a foreign land she was being terribly careless, but he gave her a pass because she didn't know she was already in hostile territory, that if Phun had already arrived, as Stewart suspected, there were now three veteran killers hunting each other in Buxton.

It was easy to see that Lenny was thrilled to be with such a beautiful woman, the kind of thing that didn't happen to him often, even though he tried hard to be popular by dressing too nicely and driving a leased

Mercedes that made locals resent him. He'd run for mayor twice but lost to a bartender and charter boat captain, respectively. He didn't have any kids or girlfriends and had never managed to fit in.

He'd once been married for eleven months, and had almost gained some measure of acceptance because of it. But that was a long time ago and ended when his wife learned he was a great deal more mediocre than he was wealthy. Since their divorce it seemed that his ex-wife's favorite hobby was sitting in bars telling embarrassing stories about the small caliber of his equipment, and his harmless but unusual ideas for sex.

The stories were a running joke in Buxton that Lenny pretended to find funny. He even repeated them on occasion, acting like he enjoyed the notoriety. Short of moving away, the man really didn't have a choice. Cruiser didn't expect him to survive long enough to live those stories down.

The two of them got into Jennifer's SUV, but Cruiser would not follow. The smart move was to wait in the shadows and listen for running footsteps or a car to start. To see who *would* follow them down the road.

There wasn't a sound or movement that didn't belong there. A diesel droned out on the water, cicadas chirped in the darkness, but no one followed Jennifer and Lenny. Phun was either not there yet or wasn't ready to play.

Of course there was the other option that Cruiser was afraid to consider. The game between them might have already started under Phun's terms, and it was never good to play by an enemy's rules. Cruiser was too smart, experienced, and jaded to overlook the possibility that at that very second, someone else might be pulling strings too.

He turned on the battery of his night-vision monocular and scanned the area slowly, leaning around the pine tree, knowing that Phun might be there doing the same thing. Phun wasn't a spy so he might be less professional, especially because of his wicked reliance on bloodthirsty violence, but he wasn't a fool.

Phun had sent Cruiser photos taken after the blast in the family's kitchen. He had boldly addressed the photos of his obliterated wife and kids to "*Sha Hai Wo Jia de Shung Shou*, Cruiser the CIA Agent," then had them delivered to the American Embassy in Beijing.

The gruesome photos were all the more horrible by the threat that came with them. *Sha Hai Wo Jia de Shung Shou* was Mandarin for "the man who murdered my family," making Stewart almost a religious target to Phun, a conflict of family honor that had to be settled in person. That sacred vow had forced Phun to the U.S. for the first time in his life, enticing him across an ocean and a continent in order to engage Cruiser in a small southern town as unfamiliar to Phun as any place could be. Which meant that Phun, too, would stay invisible.

Just before leaving his post in China, Stewart had sent copies of the photos to Trent Phillips, the sheriff in Buxton, along with the words *Sha Hai Wo Jia de Shung Shou*. He hadn't identified himself when he'd done it, but it seemed fair to give Phillips some idea of the carnage heading his town's way.

Cruiser watched as the taillights of Jennifer's SUV reached the end of the long rural road and signaled to turn left. He waited. It was silent all around.

Then an engine started and a dark Impala rolled quietly out of the parking lot.

3

Sheriff Trent Phillips was a large and naturally strong man for whom middle age affected his body very little. He'd gained a couple pounds each year, but they just made him look big, not fat – even better suited for his dominant role in Buxton's small society.

He was flopped awkwardly on the colorful futon his wife bought even though they never had guests, enjoying a bowl of ice cream and a classic movie when the phone rang.

"Trent. Robbie. I brought my Scouts back early from fishing 'cause the wind made it just a tad too rough out there."

"Should have known it with this hurricane coming."

"A bit of adventure for them, I figured. Anyway, I tied up at the boat ramp and got them on solid ground to wait for their folks to come get 'em. Wasn't two minutes before they ran back to the boat screaming about a body."

Phillips got up and instantly headed toward the door. "A human body?"

"Of course a human body. Most of one anyway."

"Don't touch anything. Ten minutes."

40

Phillips had waited most of a lifetime for this call, so long in fact that he was almost relieved to have received a package that warned it would finally happen. He'd decided right then not to do anything that could make him look scared, and so as he drove to the boat ramp he refused to use his lights or siren, rolling almost unnoticed into the parking lot.

He strolled powerfully into the ring of boys who stood just close enough to the body to stare and wonder, but not an inch closer. Then he calmly told Robbie to move them away. A few minutes later he called the local preacher.

"You'd better get down here, Marty."

"It's late."

"I've got a bunch of kids seen more than they should. Found a body with no face on it."

"A stranger?"

"Think it's Lenny but can't be sure. Don't often see something so horrible. Kids could probably use a hand and some comfort."

"Christ. Okay, Trent, I'm on my way."

The body was disfigured and shocking, but even so it didn't surprise Phillips that the Scouts kept wandering slowly back for another look. It irritated him though, because he wasn't all that sure how to investigate the crime and sure didn't need an audience. He radioed his deputy to bring some yellow evidence tape, and together they made a barrier that kept his fascinated audience watching from a distance while he shot dozens of photos of the body, the ramp, some blood on the gravel, an empty Coke can, and even one shot of the boys who discovered the body – habit forcing most of the kids to smile at the camera in spite of the circumstances. It was essential to make a good visual record of the crime scene, but far more important to look like he knew what he was doing.

After what felt like a sufficient amount of studying the body from every possible angle and a great many distances, he dug into the pockets of the dead man's trousers and found a wallet with seven dollars, along with Lenny's driver's license, several credit cards, and a picture of a young child he'd never mentioned. Then he walked around the body again in ever widening circles, expanding his search area and looking for any kind of clue, but only finding an unusual looking candy wrapper.

His deputy kept the small crowd away while Phillips sat down by the boat ramps and made careful notes about the tide, the moon, the approximate air temperature, the wind direction, and anything else he could think of, doing his best to look calm and professional as the vengeance he'd anticipated stared back at him from the bloody patch of Lenny's skull where his face had been.

Three hours later an ambulance carted off the body and Phillips, desperate for a shot of whiskey, told his deputy to guard the lot until they could examine it in the morning, and then went straight home – the only place he'd been allowed to drink since his first date with Maggie as a newly elected sheriff. They were shooting pool in Beaufort, the small town where she cleaned her dad's rental units, and he got into an argument with a fisherman. Fueled with equal parts Jack Daniels and ego, he pulled his gun on the fisherman, who was going to have him arrested until Maggie talked him out of it.

He retrieved the lone bottle of whiskey from the back of the cabinet over the refrigerator and poured himself a tumbler full, being careful not to wake Maggie because even though she was a convent-quiet kind of woman and a good wife, she tended to meddle when things were bad. That was his fault because in spite of his powerful reputation throughout eastern Carolina – or maybe because of it – he wanted his home to be a haven of irresponsibility, a place to shirk and relegate and be completely powerless.

Over the years that abdication of power had made their home a place where Maggie both ruled and managed. There was no doubt she occasionally used that power to manipulate him, but that was a small enough price to pay for a chance to be something other than sheriff whenever he was there.

By first light he was on his third heavy shot of Jack Daniels, numbly comparing the digital photos he'd taken of Lenny's body to the photos of burned and blistered corpses he'd received in the mail. They'd come all the way from China, yet even the worst of investigators could pretty well assume that the ravaged bodies in both sets of photos were connected.

He tried not to see his own dead and tortured body in a similar photo, but in the haunting shadows of early drunken hours he could not avoid catching a glimpse. The vision didn't terrify him as much as he'd always thought it would, but still he jumped when Maggie crept into the kitchen and bumped his chair. She jumped too, and then sat down and rubbed her eyes, clutching her robe against the morning's chill, looking alternately at the pictures, the liquor, and Phillips.

"Trent, what do these photos have to do with that bottle?"

"Huh?"

She didn't repeat herself and seldom did, expecting to be heard and answered the first time.

"That's Lenny. What's left of him anyway."

Maggie looked closer at the grisly photos.

"That has to hurt you. I'm sorry."

"We've been friends forever. Weren't close for years, but heck, friends since elementary school."

"Any idea who did this?"

He picked up his whiskey but she glared until he put it down. "I know exactly who did it. No doubt in my mind that a guy named Ernie Roberts killed Lenny."

"I've never even heard of him. How can you be so sure?"

"Nobody else had a reason to do this to Lenny. Now Roberts is going to make trouble for us."

"Us?"

"Me and Joe. You too, I guess. Us."

"What are you going to do?"

"I'll figure out something.'

"What's this all about?"

He hesitated, but whiskey and trust kept it short. "We killed Robert's old man."

"You killed his father?" Maggie leaned away, but after several seconds she shifted closer and cozied up, reminding him of the way she acted in sex games.

"Long time ago. A creaky old secret." He managed a weak smile.

"Well you're the sheriff, Honey. Just go out and arrest Roberts."

"Can't, even if I had enough evidence. He'd tell what we did to the papers and courts, probably saying his arrest was some weird vendetta of mine. Besides, I barely knew him, and haven't seen him in years. Not really sure where I'd find him."

"But you're sure it's him."

"I wouldn't be positive except for a bunch of photos I got in the mail and a Chinese threat to kill The Murderer of My Family. So I've got to convince Joe he's safe or else he'll go straight to the state police and tell them everything, looking for their protection. He always said that's what he'd do. He's not nearly as worried about what people think."

"Folks find out you killed a man, even if it was a long time ago, it'll cost you your job."

"I think I can stop him."

"You don't have a choice." She stood up slowly, looking around her home as if everything was suddenly at risk. "What would we do if you weren't sheriff?"

"I don't know. But I'll handle Joe. Don't worry."

"You can't watch him around the clock."

"Maybe he's changed his mind about talking. We haven't spoken about it in over a year. Ain't exactly our favorite subject."

As she calculated the damage Joe could cause, Phillips watched for her face to change when she got to the hard place he knew she was heading, a little frightened at how easily Maggie could make deadly decisions in tough times.

Her eyes settled on a small tear in the linoleum and stayed there a long time as she tightened the focus in her mind. Then she slowly looked up as though she'd worked out a solution to which there would be no reconsideration. "There's no way you can let Joe talk. And to be honest, anyone who would do that to you doesn't deserve to live anyway."

"You want me to step back and let Roberts murder Joe the way he did Lenny."

"That idiot has always followed your lead and everyone knows it, so Roberts will most likely come after you next, leaving Joe to talk behind your dead back."

45

"Roberts doesn't know I pulled the trigger. It's impossible to find a record of who did what."

"Trent," she said, her voice calmer than before, "it's clear that we're talking murder here, so you have to act. And be the first to do it."

"You mean the second. And it wasn't murder. An accident. Besides, that's what I'm going to do."

"God, you still don't understand." She rubbed his hands and spoke slowly as if educating a small child. "We can't wait to see if he kills Joe."

"You want me to lead Roberts to Joe? That's almost helping him get killed, and I'm paid to keep him safe."

"Trent, you took a *vow* to keep me safe." She looked around her precious house again. "You want to risk losing your job. Maybe work at Wal-Mart or seat people at the diner?"

"There are other things I could do."

"Building those stupid boats? Jeez, I guess I'll get to clean cabins again to make ends meet."

"It won't come to that, Maggie. I can protect Joe so he won't feel he needs to talk."

Maggie tapped a fingernail on a photo of Lenny's scalped face. "Oh yeah, I'm sure he'll feel safe once he sees how well you protected Lenny."

"Watch it, Maggie."

"He'll be scared, Trent. Who wouldn't be, so why would he risk death to protect your secret? He knows you can't protect him, so he either dies or talks, and I will not allow you to let talking be an option."

"What do you –? No! There's no way Maggie."

"He can't talk about you if he's dead."

"I won't kill my friend."

46

"Somebody's sure going to kill him, and if it's you we can put this entire thing to rest. Either way, Joe's going to die."

Maggie leaned forward until her robe fell open, then rubbed the inside of his leg. "We both know I'm right, and that you *will* do this for us."

She refilled his glass with whiskey that suddenly looked like poison. "Remember how proud I was the last time you protected me?"

*   *   *

Jay Stewart read the front page of the morning's paper while he ground some fresh coffee, not bothered at all that the word murder had long ago lost its power to faze him. But he hoped those sorts of feelings were merely damaged by his years in the trade and not dead altogether because he now had some options for his future, and he wanted any remaining seeds of those feelings to re-root themselves and grow to whatever level of beauty was possible in the years to come.

But that would take time, so the morning's shocking headlines didn't yet have the power to shock him at all. He finished the article and then set down the paper to admire his large kitchen with lots of cabinets and countertops he didn't need but enjoyed owning. Everything he owned had fit into a single cabinet, but someday he wanted to buy nice pots and pans and good silverware, stock the refrigerator with food, fill a few racks with spices, and load a shelf with cookbooks.

But killing Phun superseded that future, so he re-read the Hatteras morning paper as a civilian might, looking for insight into what other people in his new community might be feeling, clues about how to feel shocked. But it was too much to expect because on the global field in which he played, murder was nothing more than an opinion, one of several possible perspectives which were all steeped heavily in bias.

Whenever an enemy killed an American it was murder and always wrong. When we killed dozens of their people it was always necessary and just as always patriotic. If a nice old lady was murdered next door it was always senseless, and a child's murder was automatically a tragedy. Point of view meant everything, which made it suspect in all circumstances.

Other than an update on the predicted landfall of the oncoming hurricane, the front page was about nothing but Lenny's murder, eulogizing him in death with the kind of praise he'd been dying to hear while alive. It said Boy Scouts found his body at the municipal boat ramp on the Pamlico Sound, and that Lenny wasn't just murdered, but "savagely and ritualistically tortured," as the paper so colorfully described it, confirming that Lenny's face had been filleted in Phun's trademark fashion.

By letting Jennifer go back to the restaurant alone, Stewart had stepped aside and let poor Lenny draw Phun out. Lenny had taken Stewart's place as Phun's victim, making the details of Lenny's slaughter almost too personal to consider, which felt strange because there was seldom anything personal about the killings Stewart had done.

Before carrying out a sanction his target had to either make a first attack or pose a verifiably deadly threat. Stewart loathed preemptive strikes that required a guess as to his target's potential threat, and so always dug hard for proof, being an intelligence officer first and foremost with his role as a killer staying ancillary, an intricate execution of his nearly invisible job that occasionally turned deadly, but never personal.

After two cups of coffee Stewart gave up trying to guess what the average resident of Buxton might be feeling. It was a worthwhile goal and he definitely wanted to achieve it, but right now he had bigger worries than his lack of compassion for poor dead Lenny. Phun concerned him the most. Getting whatever secrets Jennifer kept from her bosses was way down the list. Packing her off to China no longer mattered.

He drove to his office and picked up the latest home listings. There were only three houses on the beach she might like, so if things didn't work out the way he planned and they did end up killing time to look at the homes, it wouldn't take long.

Part of him hoped it would work out that way, so he double-checked to make sure he had his emotions under control, and the answer was yes. Sure, he enjoyed their flirting as he dug for whatever she hid from her bosses at MI6, but there was little more to it than that. The two of them had no chance of being anything more than intellectual duelists, although he did admit to liking the way she reminded him of Simone. His life of secrecy was ending and he found himself hoping for someone else to re-occupy that tender spot from which she'd been cut away.

Of course his love for Simone was a handicap to any hopes for a new relationship, but that's the kind of scar that knife leaves.

He parked at The Lighthouse restaurant but didn't get out, trapped in a wonderful time back in Paris, and the weekend they'd taken a train to Marly, a quiet town of anonymity overlooked by the hordes of antique dealers that sprung up like mushrooms in most villages. He and Simone had looked at small farms there, and Cruiser could almost imagine leaving the Agency to start a new and honest life with her. Maybe he would learn to paint, or start a vineyard. He knew she wouldn't care if he looked silly standing in front of an easel painting bad landscapes. She brought out the silliness in him, a part of himself he loved but ignored in nearly equal proportion.

Somewhere during that time they fell in love. She was toweling dry one morning when he brought her coffee, and he just knew. He didn't know whether he first felt his love for her or hers for him, but he guarded his emotions so carefully that he figured she'd been signaling her love for a while, but not until that morning did he allow himself to feel it.

It took less than a year to prove the CIA warnings against relationships anywhere near an area of operation. On a warm evening as they sat in a great ethnic café a few blocks from Gare du Nord, a small man in a good suit walked in and immediately recognized Cruiser. He hesitated before walking to their table and saying "Monsieur Sanchez. I'm surprised to see you in Paris."

Simone looked puzzled. Cruiser stood up.

"Excuse my bad manners," the man said to Simone. "I am –"

"Let's go outside." Cruiser took the man by the arm and left.

When he returned, Simone had paid the bill and was waiting to leave. They walked half a block before she asked, "Why did he call you that name?"

Cruiser knew he should lie. Hell, his career depended on his being a good liar, but he didn't want to lie to Simone and so he said nothing. It hurt them both, and Simone sadly accepted that his silence, his unexplained absences, the locked cases he kept in their closet and how he got his money would forever be off limits. He could see in so many ways that she desperately wanted to know who he was, but mostly it showed in the way she sat quietly staring whenever he left.

That secrecy choked off their relationship as she grew to accept that his life – *that* life – was off limits, and with the insidious stealth of cancer, that harsh and sad reality gradually destroyed everything wonderful between them. He moved out and asked Nick for whatever hard mission no one else would take. Nick gave him exactly that.

Cruiser never talked to Simone again, and he never mentioned her to anyone, not even during the lost year of angry, unemployed drunkenness that followed her death and nearly caused his own. She became another of his secrets, perhaps his most precious. He would never stop cherishing her and the beautiful life she'd given him, and would forever grieve for the better life he would have had if he'd managed to keep her in it.

He liked that Jennifer reminded him of Simone, hiding so beautifully behind a seductive smile that quickly changed to innocence once she had his attention. He had sworn never to try another relationship until he left the Agency, but that barrier was eroding, so maybe he could see Jennifer as a glimpse of what he might find in his new life. It was certainly better than seeing her as such a powerful symbol of something lost.

After all, what were their chances? Jennifer was a mid-career operative struggling to build a reputation, and he already had his. Even if they ended up over-the-moon about each other, would she ever understand the peace he now craved? They were on opposite sides of success and separated by lies, secrets, and suspicion. That alone was enough to keep them apart.

He repeated their odds to himself, just to be sure.

Restaurants were valuable tools: sometimes neutral safe havens, sometimes hostile, but always public. That made them useful in many ways, so as he went into The Lighthouse to meet Jennifer he planned to use that popular local spot to its fullest.

Sheriff Phillips, sitting as usual by the corner window and picking at his food, was the unappreciative celebrity of the breakfast crowd. He was trying to have a serious talk with his deputy and Joe, the guy who owned the pier, and was obviously annoyed by the scared and curious locals who kept interrupting them. None of the three men at the table looked like they'd had much sleep.

Stewart walked over to Jennifer's table. She wore her hair down instead of in a pigtail, and when she turned to say hello he saw a large bruise on her neck.

"Good morning," she said when he got close.

"*Bonjour*." It slipped out like he was an amateur just learning the ropes, his thoughts of Simone and France causing a beginner's stumble. He tossed the newspaper onto the table and remained standing, making a big show of motioning for the waitress, attracting plenty of attention from everyone. He gave Simone's memory a final push and then went to work.

Jennifer touched his hand as he sat down, then she flashed that great smile and said "So the man who never travels speaks French? That's interesting."

"*Bonjour* and *merci*. Pretty much it. Seen this yet?" He pointed to the front-page news of last night's murder.

She glanced at the paper like she'd already read it. "No, but I knew something was wrong by the way people were acting."

The waitress poured him coffee.

"We know what we want," he said to her, "so hang on a second." Then he tapped the paper and said to Jennifer, "This is the guy you met last night at The Harpooner."

She looked closer, and did a good job of feigning surprise. "Oh my God, you're right."

The waitress ignored someone who kept calling her name.

"Has the sheriff questioned you yet? You were probably the last person to see him alive."

"You were there too."

"But I left when you went back for your keys. You must have seen him again."

He turned to the waitress. "Perhaps we do need a few more minutes to decide."

She walked quickly away.

"Just briefly. What are you suggesting?"

"Not sure. A guy I know was just murdered."

"I didn't get the impression you two were friends."

"We weren't, but murder? In this town?" He glanced at the sheriff's table to make sure the waitress was there whispering as expected.

Jennifer stared at him with an interested look, as if the box in which she'd categorized the real estate agent no longer came close to fitting.

The sheriff got up and walked over to their table, red-eyed and looking like a man who was done playing games and wanted the truth.

"Pardon me, ma'am. I'm Sheriff Phillips. Mind if I speak to you for a minute."

"Oh, hello." Her English accent seemed to pry open the sheriff's tired eyes. "Of course I don't mind."

"I understand you were with the murder victim last night."

"She was with me," Stewart said in a hurry. "We were –"

"I'm asking her, Mr. Stewart."

Stewart lowered his head like a beaten puppy.

"Yes, I was. We talked at dinner."

"The waitress at the Harpooner told me that an English woman, if you can believe that coincidence, left the restaurant with him. Would that be you?"

Stewart looked up, trying his best to look hurt and surprised.

"Yes."

"And you went where?"

"Nowhere. We said goodbye in the parking lot."

He thunked a finger to the newspaper. "But he was killed soon afterward, and no one seems to have seen him after you. You see where I'm going with this?"

"You're being ridiculous. He was a nice man and we talked a few minutes. That's all."

"I'm not buying it."

It was an interesting scene as the sheriff hovered and all the customers stared. Stewart had thrown her into the public's spotlight, which was always an uncomfortable place for a spy, but in this case probably not too dangerous of one. He could see what she was going to do, and it wasn't too far from what he would have done in the same situation if given the same bag of tools she possessed.

She rose, tiny and frail-looking against the backdrop of the big sheriff.

"I'm a five-foot-two banker who weighs seven stone six. Yet you're accusing me of hurting this poor man who was at least two times my size?"

There was a murmur throughout the restaurant as if her argument won a few people over.

"You're a terrible person!" She softened right after saying the words, playing it pretty well, using what nature gave her in such abundance. "God I'm so sorry for being rude." Then she reached out sweetly and touched Phillips' arm, being the bigger person, apparently convincing enough people of her innocence that silverware started clattering again. "I've never been questioned about a murder before. In a way it's quite exciting."

"Someone killed him and there's not a lot of folks here I haven't known all my life. You happen to be one of them so I had to ask." Sheriff Phillips looked like he'd never really had any faith in his accusation either. Then he threw Stewart a "and you're another one" look, then went back to his table and wrote notes on a pad.

Jennifer sat quietly and looked like she was trying hard to think of anything she could tell the sheriff that might help him find the killer. But Stewart knew she was fuming. Then she stood up slowly and in a voice loud enough for most people could hear said, "You were there too. Perhaps *you're* the one who killed him."

"I've got to wonder what happened after I left you two alone."

Jennifer walked out while the locals looked back and forth between them.

* * *

55

Sheriff Phillips hoped he'd made a good impression on the locals by going through the motions of questioning the British woman, even though it was nothing but obligation, chasing the lead the waitress had provided even though he knew she hadn't done a damned thing. There was no doubt in his mind that Ernie Roberts killed Lenny. There was nothing more mysterious to it than that.

Joe went back to yakking nervously into his ear while the locals looked ready for him to make a speech, so after a few minutes he threw ten bucks on the table and walked out. He drove toward the ferry to Ocracoke, wanting to get across the sound and back before they shut down for the hurricane.

In his twenty-plus years of police work, Phillips had learned plenty about serial killers. He'd studied them at the F.B.I.'s National Academy, and a few years back had helped investigate the Campus Killer of Durham. The knowledge he'd gained was sure to come in handy as he figured out how to stay alive and out of his own jail. Although Lenny was the only person to die so far, he already knew it was essential for this to spiral into a serial killer scenario, with the only variable being the names of the victims.

As he drove through the quiet streets of Hatteras Village, he was almost thankful for his own experiences as a murderer, even though only the second one had actually been planned. The first time he'd killed, the one for which he was now dealing with the consequences, had been purely accidental.

It hadn't been precise or methodical like Lenny's death, and in fact wasn't really murder at all. The court had ruled that Phillips lacked intent to commit murder when he, Lenny, and Joe broke into the Roberts home to steal the old man's coin collection, planning to sell it to buy a car. The family was supposed to be out of town, so it shocked the hell out them when Mr. Roberts came down the stairs with a shotgun as Lenny and Joe drank from his bar.

Because Phillips had been more determined to find the coins, he was busy searching the study when he heard Roberts shouting at them to put their hands up. He sneaked up behind Roberts, but as he got close the old man heard him and spun around with the shotgun. That's when Phillips instinctively shot him with his dad's .357. It was all such a bad mistake, a minor theft that accidentally turned deadly.

Phillips's dad was the town's chief of police, but he did his job and arrested the boys the same way he would anybody else. He talked at length to the county prosecutor, of course, and had the judge over for dinner a few times, but only to make sure the case remained in their jurisdiction. It was hard enough for the boys to keep up with their schoolwork, he argued, and if the court eventually found them innocent of murder – which he was sure they would – what a shame if they were held back a grade because they'd missed too much school to the trial.

The prosecutor finally decided not to press charges against any of the boys, and Chief Phillips promptly made certain the records were sealed and ultimately destroyed. No one ever revealed the boys' names to the press.

Now that Lenny was dead, there was no doubt at all that Roberts's son Ernie would do his best to kill him and Joe. At breakfast the people of Buxton had shown him just how terrified they were of who might be the next victim, but Phillips knew they were all as safe as they'd ever been. As with any smart lawman in a small town, Phillips understood that the law was whatever he said it was, so all he had to do was invent a reason to kill Roberts before Roberts got him or Joe, and it would all be over. He'd been around long enough to know that everybody gets cut in a knife fight, so he certainly expected some damage as he worked to survive, but if he played smart and cool, he would live and keep his secret.

He thought it odd that his next and possibly last lethal victim would be the son of his first, but if that was the way things worked out, fine.

* * *

Stewart slowly finished his breakfast and then went back to his house to call Langley. He had a good view of the ocean as he talked to his boss in the same relaxed manner he'd used with him for years, trusting Nick as much as he trusted anyone in an organization of professional liars. They exchanged information like friendly experts, probing for the truth in each other's facts but careful about what they revealed in their own, and doing it all over secure phone lines.

"I can only make a guess about who leaked your whereabouts, Cruiser. That kind of thing doesn't happen often, but when it does it's usually the same. Someone undervalued the information and that led them to treat it carelessly. I doubt they intended to help Phun find you."

"What does my replacement think?"

"His sources in China confirm that Phun knows where you are."

"That's just perfect. What are you going to do to stop him?"

"Nothing. Of course, he's looking for Cruiser and not Jay Stewart, so that might keep you alive."

"Can't you intercept him at a border? Code him as a terrorist or something?"

"Too late for that. A dollar says he's already there, probably watching you right now."

"Who do you think gave me up?"

"That's the mystery. I'd guess it was someone here at headquarters. The guy who took over for you is too much of a pro, handpicked by me. Closest I had to someone of your caliber."

"Don't stroke me."

"Wouldn't think of it. And the person who's partnering up with him is still down in your neck of the woods. Speaking of which, have you ..." he cleared his throat and affected a British accent..."cast a butcher's at her yet? Introduced yourself?"

"The Brit? Yes and no."

"Give me the yes."

"I've seen her."

"And the no?"

"She hasn't made me yet."

"You've got to be enjoying that."

"I guess she bought all our dis-information. Where's her distrust of everything official? Doesn't Vauxhall Cross teach cynicism anymore?"

"She's plenty cynical, but even half the folks who work here at Langley believe that description of you, so why shouldn't she?"

"She's not good enough to go after Phun. She'll get herself killed for nothing."

"She's been good enough so far...wait a minute. What was that tone in your voice just now? I've heard it once before."

"Don't be an idiot."

"Hmm. Well, you know how well she did in the Royal Marines and MI5, so don't underestimate her. And I've only recently learned that since her move to MI6 she's made five confirmed kills, two as covert assassinations with the Red Sabbath Guard."

"Jeez, the guys who take body parts as souvenirs?"

"That's them."

"Hard to see her doing that."

"Word is she's tough in a fight."

"Why doesn't her agency trust her?"

"I think they trust her. It just bothers them that everyone else qualified to go after Phun ran the other way. Which makes perfect sense because it's damned near a death sentence."

"You didn't say that when you assigned the case to me."

"Not a death sentence for someone like you. Anyway, she fought for the chance to go after that animal. Demanded the opportunity. That kind of enthusiasm breeds worry. But she's fluent in Mandarin and doesn't back down from a fight, so she probably sees it as a chance to showcase her ability."

"And she's Red Sabbath? Did not know that."

"New day, something new to learn. So help her however you can and then send her packing so she can interdict Phun's other plans. You're at the top of his hit list but don't think he's forgotten we sunk his freighter, or the reasons he hated us in the first place. He has at least two other attacks in the works, and she needs to get over there and help your replacement stop them."

"In a few days."

"Two days. That's an order."

"I might be able to find out if she's hiding anything in two days, but it would take two weeks to humble her enough to fit in over there. She's too green. Heck, last night she thought the local insurance guy was Cruiser. She went after him like a fish to a lure."

"Nothing happens by accident when you're involved. I'm sure you set the stage, so don't be too hard on her. Remember when you convinced the F.B.I. that I was an Iraqi mole?"

"You're not? I'm still not sure."

"I've got scars from their handcuffs, the bastards."

"It was funny. God, that one agent almost shot you when –"

"All I'm saying is you're a great manipulator. Maybe she isn't as experienced as you, but I'm asking you to give her a break. You played the Bureau against me, so I wouldn't expect you to judge too harshly her falling for your misdirection, especially since she has the same information about you as Phun."

"She's cocky."

"I hear she's a looker."

"Probably why she's cocky. Any advice regarding Phun?"

"Don't get killed. If you do get killed, be nice to me in your will."

"Are the Feds aware of Phun?"

"No, and I don't plan to tell them because they'd be all over us about jurisdiction. With Phun on fire he needs to be dead or played, not arrested, and my life is less complicated if that's done in China."

"You make him sound easy. You forget that I already failed at killing him?"

"Okay, so maybe we can just play him when he goes back home. At the minimum we should be able to keep him from succeeding with his attacks. This guy has the money and resources to kill millions of Americans. After he kills you, of course."

"And you inherit my money."

"And I inherit your money. Right. See ya."

Stewart hung up and went out on his deck, twelve feet off the ground and high above the dunes. From there he could check the surf for a mile in either direction, all the way from the small shore break to the bigger waves breaking outside.

The strengthening onshore wind toppled the waves into soup while a couple of surfers did their best to make something out of them, paddling left or right or farther out whenever a set of waves formed up. Every once in a while their efforts paid off and they were in the right spot to catch a wave when it jacked up.

And that was the secret to life, being in the right place at the right time. Stewart had usually been lucky that way. There were also times when he'd been in the wrong place at exactly the wrong time, but because he needed his life to be a thrill ride he accepted those bad drops and scary turns without question or anguish. They were the price tag, but years of writing the checks had never settled the bill for what he'd done in Nicaragua.

So whenever his mind took him to that dark memory he tried to paste a right place / right time event over top of it. If that didn't conceal his brutality on that violent muggy night, usually it disguised it a little.

His memory of surfing the hurricane was the good event he used most often. She'd been ripping up the entire Eastern seaboard when he and two fraternity brothers drove from Chapel Hill to the southern end of Hatteras Island. They parked in the lot of Cape Hatteras Lighthouse and got out of their car, but the wind was so strong that his buddies climbed right back in, telling Stewart it was a wasted trip and that they should go back to the hurricane parties at home.

It was impossible to see over the dunes but the pounding noise offered deafening proof that the ocean had churned itself into something vicious that seduced a daring yet terrified part of Cruiser's soul, demanding that he be part of whatever danger waited for him on the other side of the dune.

He un-strapped his board and was twice pushed to the ground as he struggled along the boardwalk, saying "I won't let this scare me" over and over in an effort to convince himself it was true. When he got over the dune, he didn't dare look at the ocean.

Foam as high as his waist blew along the beach as he attached the surfboard's leash to his ankle. At the water's edge he looked at the ocean for the first time and said "Oh my God" before he could stop the fearful words.

The Atlantic was a monstrous nightmare of white water with steep, black faces. The wind held the waves up for so long they didn't look like they would ever break, and when they finally did curl over they cascaded millions of gallons of water from so high up that it formed a barrel large enough to drive a truck through. Panic tore at his mind and ripped at his nerves. It was foolish and perhaps suicidal to go out there to drown or be crushed, and there was no hope at all of a rescue.

He took three steps into the water and the rip current instantly swept him off his feet and bounced him along the bottom. He clambered onto his board and paddled like a madman into the giant washing machine gone insane. It took an hour to get outside and into the lineup a quarter mile offshore. His arms ached and his shoulders screamed but if he rested he would start shivering and his muscles would cramp.

A big wave rolled menacingly under him, lifting him twenty feet higher into the air and letting him see the two waves behind it. He paddled as fast as he could and punched his board through the top of the second wave, then fell all the way to the surface. The impact hurt but he ignored it and paddled like crazy up the face of the third wave. It lifted him until he spun his board around, looked left and right for the best direction, and then took off toward the bottom.

The wave was too steep and hollow and his fin slipped free of the water, sending him freefalling to the bottom where tons of water collapsed on him and pushed him under, deeper and deeper into the darkness, forcing him to equalize several times before he hit bottom. His leash snapped, leaving him disoriented and completely alone twenty feet or more under water, unable to follow his leash which would have kept his surfboard tombstoning at the surface.

When he finally found the surface the water was so thick with foam that he couldn't breathe. He pushed it away, sucked hard for clear air, and noticed that the sun had broken through in spots and changed the sky, making him feel like he'd been underwater every bit as long as it felt.

He swam toward shore, knowing he would get injured and maybe killed as each wave tossed him to the bottom, so he looked back to gauge when the next wave would hit and saw his surfboard pop out of the ocean a hundred feet farther out to sea.

It was terrifying to think about swimming away from the beach in those conditions, but he forced himself toward the angry, snarling monster of water that growled in low tones as it chewed up the ocean and headed toward his board. He beat it to the spot, catching his board as a thirty foot wave loomed up like it intended to crush him.

He made two lame strokes, expecting the screaming offshore wind to blow him over the back, but just then the wave's power picked him up and launched him forward, accelerating him faster than ever before. As he managed to stand up, the surfboard almost sped out from under him as he made the big drop to the bottom with the board slapping the water so hard and fast it became wildly unstable, just an inch of the tail and the fin in the water, offering no resistance at all.

He forced himself to do the unthinkable and leaned forward in order to accelerate even more as the wave crashed around him, covering him several times over in spraying white water as he made a high-compression bottom turn that almost buckled his knees before getting the board turned to cruise along the enormous wave.

He rode it forever. At one point he even shot up to the lip and made a gutsy cutback as a slap in the wave's face, a necessary penance for his being terrified by it earlier. As the wave crashed into shallower water it weakened, and he rode it into the shore break where it hollowed out again and gave him a quick little tube ride.

He hit the beach and wanted to kiss it, very much glad to be alive. The rain had stopped and the sky had cleared. A week seemed to have passed since he'd paddled out.

His friends ran down to him like legless torsos moving through the shroud of brown foam that blew along the beach. They were so excited he could barely understand what they were saying. One of them had taken pictures. "Oh, man," they said over and over, "that was so awesome."

During the ride back to Chapel Hill, Stewart asked them to keep what he'd done a secret. Tell the story if you want, and show the pictures. Just don't tell anyone it was me, at least not while I'm around.

It was impossible for them to understand, but they agreed.

The hurricane had given him the shiniest moments of his life, and now, as he planned to slaughter Phun in a sickening pattern he had no choice but to follow, he saw a fresh opportunity in the new hurricane heading across the Atlantic toward Hatteras.

If he timed things right he could use it to his advantage and then wash himself clean. The ripping waters of a violent ocean would make what he'd done to Phun insignificant, earning him a new good memory for whenever Phun's tortured face came back to haunt him.

As Stewart looked out on the ocean from his porch he wondered if the surf might be a little better down the coast where the island curved west and the wind would hold up the wave faces. He looked north toward the Buxton Lighthouse that played so prominently in his past and wondered about that break.

But he still wasn't ready to surf.

He made a sandwich for later and then went to the office, where he pretended at being a Realtor by fiddling with stuff on his desk. All the while he tried not to look over his shoulder for Phun, an Asian in a southern town, a man whom Stewart had very little chance of seeing anyway.

4

Doing nothing when there was nothing to be done was often the hardest part of the job. So as Stewart's complex plan played out with either his life or a tortured death on the line, he sat idly in his office reminding himself that everything was on schedule and therefore doing nothing was the professional thing to do.

He intended to mix Phun's death into the swirl of bad news surrounding the hurricane, which meant its arrival, regardless of how powerfully it came ashore, was zero hour. He'd worked everything backward from then after checking and rechecking all the possible weather sources and adjusting his schedule to match the changes.

It was still too early to tip off Phun that he'd wasted the secrecy of his presence by killing Lenny, so unless Phun accelerated the timetable by trying to leave town, Stewart would wait until late this afternoon to give him the truth, and that meant he could concentrate on Jennifer, who was temporarily, by design, a higher priority than Phun. That gave him no choice but to wait for her to burst through the door and either demand or elicit some answers about what he'd done to her at breakfast. It was the predictable reaction for a tough career spy who'd been sidetracked by a civilian.

But she didn't do that, and so every minute he waited forced him to question if she was more or less skillful than he'd figured. Was it possible she'd somehow discovered he needed her? Did she have any clue to what he was doing? Or was it possible she was being unpredictable just to act as a "normal" woman might predictably act? He gamed all those scenarios and their logical extensions, all the while placing reasonable confidence in his ability to manipulate even a pro like Jennifer.

But the skill of an excellent marksman was of little use in a knife fight, so was it possible that he and Jennifer were in different kinds of fights? Was she up to more than he'd figured, and if so, had he assigned too much importance to her need to find Cruiser without asking for help?

She finally walked in at exactly five o'clock, as though she'd waited until closing because it fit neatly into some game of her own design, a game Stewart would have to quickly figure out and counter. She smiled at the receptionist but didn't stop at her desk as she slid past. Stewart would have had an impossibly hard time taking his eyes off her as he got into character, so he didn't bother.

"Hi, got a minute to talk?"

"I'm pretty busy right now." He kept filling out the dummy listing.

She sat down anyway, gracefully using her legs as a powerful tool that Stewart would not allow to work on him.

"May I?"

"Of course. Chair isn't all that comfortable though."

"Why did you do that to me this morning? Just curious."

"I said I was sorry."

"It seemed so intentional, but you don't seem like a cruel person."

"I was just asking if you'd seen the paper."

"I really loved how you kept the waitress there listening. What was it you said? 'We know what we want so stay here a second.' Something like that"

"I was hungry."

"And now I can't help but wonder why I was given your name to be my estate agent?"

"That sounds like a question for whoever gave it to you."

"They thought it might have come from an MLS website."

"Then there you have it. Was there something else?"

"Not really. Ready to show me some houses then?"

"We were supposed to do it this morning."

"By the way, I went to the website. Your name isn't listed there."

"It's probably being updated or changed."

She leaned forward and reached for his hand, then whispered as if they were in on his secret together. "You've never actually sold a house, have you?"

He patted her hand and whispered back, "Maybe I was holding out so you could be my first." Then he squared the stapler with his inbox and straightened the other items on his desk, anything he could find to put both hands to work.

"In that case I can't help but be fascinated that you got your name out there so well that it was given to me. Maybe you could teach me how so that I could promote myself at the bank. So if you had to guess, how do you think I got it?"

"Okay, I'll take a stab at that, for your career at the bank."

"Thank you."

"I bet someone in the military provided it. Or law enforcement."

"You're answering my question by guessing?"

Now was the time to press, to work toward whatever she might be hiding from MI6, any kind of agenda she might have outside the scope of her mission to kill Phun and interdict his attacks on the U.S. and Great Britain.

"I'll even bet it was someone pretty high up," he continued. "Tell me who and I'll tell you how."

"I don't know anything about him."

"So you're in the habit of following advice from men you know nothing about?"

"He was a guy my brother met when he came here to fish. A soldier, I think."

"Well that certainly makes it easy. You see, I was in Army for twenty years, stationed most of that time not far from here at Fort Bragg. I sent everyone I know a card when I retired last year. Sounds like one ended up in his hands."

"I'm not sure I believe that."

He got up and headed toward the door, pretty sure she would give chase. "I'm not sure I care."

"Where are you going? I thought we were talking."

"Then talk to me over a drink. I'll even let you buy because I've never sold a house."

He climbed into his Jeep and backed up, expecting Jennifer to race to her car and follow before he got out of sight. But she surprised him by jumping into his moving car as he was pulling out of the parking lot. Neither of them spoke as they drove two miles to a bar next to the fishing pier. The sheriff's car was in the parking lot.

"I can take us somewhere else if you're afraid of the sheriff. Nervous, I mean. Could be awkward inside."

"For whom? I still think you might have been the one to kill Lenny, so let's both go in and have that drink."

She got out of the car and walked ahead of Stewart into the locals' joint that served beer by the pitcher and oysters by the bucket. Jimmy Buffett sang about island drinks from dusty speakers and fishermen shot pool in the back. All eyes immediately settled on Jennifer as they stood in the doorway, making hers a terribly uncomfortable spot for anyone.

"Please," she said, far less confident than a minute earlier but possibly by design, "let's just sit down."

He stayed planted in the doorway and gave the crowd a few more seconds. With no other suspects popping up during the day, he wanted them to think that the sheriff had been right at breakfast, that she'd had something to do with Lenny's death after all. If they didn't yet, he knew they soon would.

No one looked friendly, nor did anyone feel the need to whisper the rumor to someone who might be unaware. Even the men just back from fishing seemed to suspect her of murder, standing silently with beers in their hands and awestruck looks on their faces, their attraction to her beauty thrown off by their fear of what she might have done.

"Sure," he said, as he realized that the patrol car outside must belong to the sheriff's deputy. "We'll sit anywhere you like."

"How about this table right here?"

"The bar's a lot better."

"But I'd rather –"

"Trust me." He took her hand and led her to the bar on the far side of the room, needing to shatter any hopes she had of controlling the game, and forcing her to worry about what he might do.

At one end of the short bar sat an old man and at the other was Joe, a nice little friend of the sheriff who owned

71

the adjoining fishing pier. There were five empty stools between them, and since Stewart had noticed that Joe was the only guy who didn't look at Jennifer when they'd stood in the door, he wanted to know why.

"How about here?" He pulled out the stool next to Joe and waited for her to sit.

"Another trick like at breakfast?"

"It's just better down at this end. Right Joe?"

Joe turned so unsteadily that he might have been drinking ever since his breakfast with Sheriff Phillips, which would explain why he'd missed Jennifer's entrance. For the small part he was to play in Stewart's plan to use Jennifer, Joe's drunkenness would actually help.

As Joe focused on Stewart and Jennifer he raised his hand and pointed a weaving finger in their general direction. "My God it's you!"

"Don't be rude, Joe. She had nothing to do with Lenny's death so leave her alone."

"I knew it was you all along. Now you've come for me, haven't you?"

"Right, Joe, she came all the way from England for you. Beer for me," he said to the bartender. "Jennifer?"

He watched in the bar's mirror as Joe's shaky finger wandered around in the air.

Stewart was pretty sure he'd already gotten Jennifer frustrated enough for some of it to leak out if she felt she had the latitude, and so if she didn't react it meant she was onto him and working like a professional, unwilling to show any anger that served no purpose.

But it was precisely that pressure to stay cool when required that made it rewarding to vent when given the chance, so whichever way she went, he'd have an answer.

After several seconds of watching Joe's finger weave around in front of her face she said, "You're being rude, my cute little friend, and if you're still pointing in my direction in two seconds I'm taking that finger. One ..."

Joe didn't seem to hear her, but Stewart had his answer. She was willing to use her professional training in an unprofessional way, so she certainly didn't feel like she was in a game of any real significance. She still didn't know he was Cruiser.

"And that's two," she said as she snatched Joe's finger, cranked it back, and then lifted him off his stool with it as the bar went silent and Joe stared wide-eyed.

Stewart eased off his stool as if diffusing a bomb, making sure he didn't block the view of what was happening from the locals. "Okay, you'd better cool down, Jennifer. This guy's a little drunk but you're way out of line."

She cracked the finger back until it broke with a loud pop. People groaned and the bartender told her to quit, but Joe couldn't manage to say anything.

"Sorry about this," Stewart said to the bartender.

"I want that killer out of here."

"Piss off," she said sweetly, and then walked through the bar and out the door as the deputy straightened his gun belt and shouted "You shouldn't leave town until the sheriff gets back."

Joe wandered back to the guys playing pool, holding out his hand with the busted finger. One of the guys said "Man, you really showed her" and laughed as he broke the rack.

Stewart shrugged at the bartender and ordered another beer. He would drink very slowly, strategically putting lots of time between himself and Jennifer before going to work on Phun.

* * *

After all the mistakes she'd made since her arrival in Buxton, Jennifer was lucky that her car and the bar were within walking distance. It felt like the only thing she hadn't done badly since her arrival, which had the natural effect of forcing her to search for the moment she'd suddenly turned incompetent.

She'd come to North Carolina full of well-earned confidence, expecting to quickly find the legendary Cruiser, dazzle him a bit for good measure, and then get the information she needed for her mission in China. After that it would be a race to Beijing to kill Phun before someone else did it, further advancing her reputation that competed directly with Cruiser's by accomplishing the only task he'd ever failed to do.

But her day had started with Jay Stewart making her a murder suspect, and she'd just replaced the tiny woman image that might have saved her at breakfast with a violent display of her hurting the drunk. Stewart must have set up to accuse her at the bar, and she'd fallen for it. She'd trumped her own hand and muddied her party dress, as her mum would say.

She wanted to believe that Stewart was unaware of what he'd done to her, and failing that she wanted to believe she'd handled him carelessly because up until breakfast he'd done very little to wiggle her antennae. Either option was palatable but neither was the truth.

For some reason she couldn't fathom, Jay Stewart, the retired Army soldier turned estate agent, had gamed her better than anyone else in her covert life. That meant he must have gotten some guidance, which meant he was most likely working with Cruiser, which indicated that he was probably helping Cruiser, perhaps being the public figure behind which Cruiser could effectively hide.

The more she walked along and strung those beads together, the more it all made sense. After all, she'd seen several black people since she'd arrived in Buxton, but except for Lenny, none came close to fitting the description she'd been given of Cruiser. That meant he was in deep hiding, so of course he would need help. Jay Stewart had well served Cruiser's purpose, probably better than Cruiser could ever have hoped he would.

She was angry for having been played, but mostly with herself because she was the professional, not Stewart. Accepting the blame actually gave her room to admire what he'd managed to do, even if he'd had Cruiser's guidance. She had no clues about Stewart's motives, but whatever they were, he'd done to her what she usually did to others. She couldn't help but be impressed because seldom had anyone made her such an easy mark. Had she made it simple by trusting him intuitively when they'd met at the house?

It was a deep flaw in her nature to trust people and she was always inclined to do it – a severe handicap in her line of work and the very reason she stayed so faithfully on guard against it. She shouldn't have relaxed around him, but she knew why she had and that made it easier to defend against in the future. There was something about Stewart she liked, which meant she should have known he was bad for her. Her instincts about men always worked out that way, so the only way to trust her instincts now was as a warning sign.

She certainly wasn't a sucker for guys, at least not anymore, but if there was a type of man to whom she was vulnerable it was someone like Stewart with a successful past that didn't control his present, a man perfectly content not to broadcast the strengths he must necessarily have, thereby allowing whatever made him strong to show up in quiet confidence. Beyond that it should stay deep and hidden and almost mysterious.

She couldn't help but be intrigued by men like that, which always got her thinking about the loneliness to which she seldom admitted. With Stewart her intrigue was compounded by his choice of towns, since he probably could have chosen to retire anywhere but picked a town very much like the one in her own fantasies of her future, fantasies she knew would grow to obsessions once she managed to kill Phun so she could get on with her life.

She deserved to be hard on herself over Stewart, but she would forgive herself for attacking the drunk because she never allowed herself much choice in those situations. She would use only her beauty at times when she totally controlled the game, or in the impossibly rare relationship with an honest man, but whenever she played a man's game – which she did all the time – she played shot for shot by a man's rules. It was necessary to survive and the only way to prove herself equal. Anything short of equality was subservience, at least to her, and she would never be submissive unless it was merely a role she played briefly in a game of her choosing.

A mile or so from the bar she stopped near a Dairy Queen and dialed London from her cell phone.

"Listening," said a man's voice.

"This is nine-triple-four. I might have located my target on the Outer Banks but I have doubts. He was black, driving a Mercedes, and running a local insurance agency. A perfect match for the description Langley gave us." She double-checked the lighted diode on the scrambler and made sure it was still green.

"Did you talk to him yet?"

"Last evening. As you suggested I'm pretending to look for a house, using the recommended estate agent for information and access. He introduced us at dinner."

"If he is Cruiser, be careful. His history makes him impossible to predict, so take it slow pushing for an ident."

"He was murdered last night and a thumb was cut off."

"Red Sabbath?"

"Sounds like it. You didn't send anyone else did you?"

"Of course not. And since you're the only RS there I have to ask if you did it. Cruiser was one of the best, so if you killed him I need to know in order to handle the CIA and get you off to China."

"I didn't kill Cruiser."

"But an ear was missing?"

"A thumb."

"A token, same thing."

"I don't think the guy really was Cruiser. He might have been his brother or something, but he wasn't smart enough. And he was too entrenched in this town to have returned just a few months ago. Cruiser's still out there. If he's all that intelligent and unique, he'll stand out here."

"He's survived for decades by not standing out. I could check with Langley for better information. It's not too late."

She checked her surroundings. The sun had set but there was still plenty of light. A family ate ice cream at a metal table in the shade, but no one was nearby.

"The estate agent will lead me to him. But even if he doesn't I'd have to be *completely* incompetent to miss a legendary spy in this town of three hundred carrot-crunching Swede bashers."

"That kind of cockiness almost kept you off this assignment. Don't compromise yourself and don't waste time. You know there's a clock ticking. Back-channel chatter indicates that Phun's nearly ready with a new attack."

"I'll find Cruiser."

She hesitated, wanting to tell her boss that Phun was also in Buxton, and that MI6's clock was now ticking on Eastern U.S. time. She could be fired for withholding the information, and criminally prosecuted if it enabled Phun to attack either country by surprise.

"One last time. You're sure you didn't make the kill last night?"

"Don't be ridiculous."

"Then get to work. Let me know when you find him."

She hung up without saying anything else, unplugged her scrambler and stuck it in her purse, still worrying about her omission of facts. If Phun really thought Lenny was Cruiser, then he believed his business in America was finished, that he'd killed the man who killed his family. He would go back to China and become invisible once again.

Worse yet, something was terribly wrong with her emotions, and the weakness of being human was tearing at her for the first time.

She knew she couldn't let Phun leave the island, and at the same time she hoped to God he was already gone.

* * *

Sheriff Phillips spent the day in Ocracoke, the island just south of Hatteras where he always went to think like a criminal. Its location had provided Blackbeard the pirate with quick access to ships following the trades up the coast, and something about that history kept drawing Phillips back.

He was on the ferry crossing Pamlico Sound when Joe called whining about the English woman breaking his finger. Joe was right to be afraid, but of Ernie Roberts, and not of her.

It felt a little careless to be so sure of himself so early in an investigation where his only solid clue was a wrapper from candy made in England, but hadn't Roberts personally threatened him by sending that package of horrible photos to his office? Roberts' name wasn't on it, of course, but mailing it to *the murderer who killed my family* said it all. Anyone unfamiliar with their tangled past might never have guessed it, but it was obvious as the sun to him.

Joe's call made him wonder if Roberts and the English woman were a team. For all he knew she might even be his wife or girlfriend. He needed to deal with Roberts alone, so he would get her out of the way by using the town's assumption of guilt to isolate her.

Maggie had insisted that he controlled who died, and he'd agreed to be just as precise and methodical in his killing of Joe as Roberts was with Lenny. That would establish a pattern, and that would allow him to hide the truth forever by claiming that Lenny, Joe and Roberts were all murdered by someone who'd drifted into town and then moved on. If the locals didn't relax after a few months, Phillips would go to Virginia or South Carolina and duplicate the crimes, proving absolutely that the murderer was no longer around Buxton.

He would have a hard time slicing off slabs of his friend's cheeks and ripping off his thumb, and then sliding a thin knife so deep into his ear that it hit the other side of his skull. Extensive bleeding indicated that Lenny had been alive during the entire filleting ritual, and the ragged flesh at the stump of his thumb indicated that it had been torn off, which made it more sickening to think about. But Phillips was a survivor who would not disgrace his wife or hamstring his son for whom he wanted life to be so much better.

"John," he'd said just last week as they ate lunch by the harbor, "you see old man Fischer's wooden boat out there at anchor?"

"Sure."

"I helped him build it."

"You're kidding."

"No. When I was just about your age he hired me for a summer and that's what we built."

"That's so cool."

Phillips loved boats so much he still daydreamed about designs, but he avoided them for the same reason an alcoholic avoids a bar.

"You sure you want to be a cop, John?"

"You're one. Granddad was. It's tradition."

"Sure seems to be. But if I'd ever had the guts to stand up to my old man I would have built boats. Custom flats boats, you know, good for shallow waters but able to handle a decent chop."

"I suppose that could be interesting."

"My dad gave me no choice in the matter, so make sure you know you have one."

Phillips had helped build Fischer's boat the same year he'd killed Ernie Roberts' dad, and for all the years since he'd hoped Roberts had died somewhere, maybe in a traffic accident or one of the wars fought since then. When his widowed mother moved away to Florida, Phillips thought the whole thing might be over. But he never stopped looking over his shoulder. Lenny, on the other hand, had tried to forget what they'd done, and that's what got him killed.

If Phillips was single and alone he might handle this differently, but his wife didn't deserve the pain of dealing with this and his son didn't deserve to be tainted by his father's past sins.

The building winds forced the ferry captain to charge the dock and bang his vessel hard into the pilings. Phillips drove off slowly and passed through Hatteras Village. He turned down Joe's long driveway that separated two big homes as it wound its way to a pie-shaped lot on the water. Joe bought all the land years ago and broke it into three lots, then sold the front two parcels to pay back the loan, keeping the best piece, a two-acre point of land, for him to build a tiny home for him and a cottage for his mother. Over the last twenty years he'd planted trees along the drive and hedges along the fences. It was as private as it was beautiful.

Joe was sitting on his front porch with his machete beside him. He didn't look drunk anymore. The lawnmower was out, but the grass hadn't been mowed except around his mother's cottage. It was freshly cut and the flowerbeds manicured. Joe had taken care of her for so long that it was first nature, even when he'd been drinking. The work probably sobered him up.

"Hey," Phillips said as he stepped onto the porch. "How's the finger?"

"Hurts."

Phillips grinned like Joe was being a sissy. "Got a cold one in the fridge? Want one?"

"Not me. Help yourself."

Phillips went through Joe's neat home, which wasn't any bigger than a doublewide trailer. It was big on character, though, with tongue and groove ceilings and floors, a stone fireplace, and a built-in glass-fronted cabinet full of crystal. Phillips grabbed two beers and walked out the back door, then ambled around the porch that wrapped the house. "I need this," he said when he got back to the front. "Drink with me."

Joe hesitated before he took the beer. Then he stood up, walked to the corner of the porch and looked over the water that lapped at the rear yard.

"I should have sold this place and moved Momma away years ago. I always knew Roberts would come back to haunt us."

"I wasn't so sure." Phillips picked off a tiny piece of white paint that had started to peel.

"Don't do that. You sure now?"

"Yeah, I'm sure. But just because Roberts is here doesn't mean he's going to beat us."

"Did a number on Lenny."

"Lenny wasn't expecting an attack."

"I ain't even got a gun around here." Joe jabbed his beer toward the chair where he'd left his machete. "Out here like some damn bushman going to fight him off with that thing. Shoot, talk about stupid."

Phillips picked up the machete and pretended to threaten Joe with it. "You want to borrow a gun? Got plenty."

Joe looked like he wanted to say yes, but he turned away and checked the water again. "No, thanks. Learned my lesson about guns a long time ago, so I'll just take my chances with that cane-cutter there. It'll probably get me killed, but I ain't gonna chance killing someone innocent."

"I'm telling you he wasn't innocent. Old man Roberts would have killed us that night."

"You don't know that."

"Were you going to stand there and wait for the police to arrive?"

"I was gonna run."

"And right there is when he'd have shot you. I saved your life, so to speak, so stop acting like this is my fault. Hell, even if Roberts does kill you, I bought you lots of extra years."

Joe's eyes opened wide but he didn't say anything.

"Let me see where she hurt your finger."

"No."

He stabbed the machete at it and nicked Joe's hand. "Damn, Joe, sorry. Let me get you a bandage out of the car."

"No big deal. Get cut all the time on the pier."

"I didn't expect it to be so sharp. Should have known better." He walked off the porch to his car, and a minute later returned with a first aid kit. "At least let me clean it up for you."

Joe looked touched as Phillips doctored him.

"I guess you'll live, so come on, let's finish these beers and go check on that English gal. If we're lucky we might catch her roughing up kids on the playground."

"It's not funny, Trent. I don't mind admitting I'm scared."

"Ah, hell, I won't let him get you. Grab the rest of that six-pack and let's go."

"Can't remember the last time I saw you drink away from home."

Phillips opened his mouth but couldn't find words worth saying. He walked to the car and opened the trunk. As Joe locked up his house, Phillips took out one of the two fillet knives he'd bought in Ocracoke. He carefully wiped it with the cotton ball he'd just used to clean Joe's wound. The fresh blood made a bright smear next to the dull sample of Lenny's blood he got at the autopsy. He closed the trunk and stuck the knife under his seat.

* * *

Phun sat on the bed of his motel room in the tiny town of Salvo and admired the thumb of his victim. He'd flown from Los Angeles to Charlotte, mystified by security that checked his shoes but not his fingerprints and scanned him for metal but didn't search for ceramic knives that were just as sharp and every bit as deadly.

Not that any of it mattered. He'd never been fingerprinted and hadn't carried anything suspicious on the plane, but it just seemed odd that he could travel so freely to anywhere he had the desire and courage to go – two emotions in absolute conflict because he had plenty of courage but little desire to visit North Carolina other than to kill Cruiser. Now that he'd done that, he could go home.

His travel documents weren't under his name but were certainly genuine, worn from frequent examination by both Chinese and U.S. Immigration. He got them by killing an exporter who traveled extensively between the two countries, and then had supporting papers professionally done under a matching name. Short of a thorough investigation there was no way he would be discovered, and as long as he stayed innocuous there would be no reason for any agency to be thorough.

It had been surprisingly easy to find and kill the legendary Cruiser. As so often happened, reputation was far larger than reality. Cruiser had been so weak and terrified and shameful that he'd actually disappointed Phun, who wanted to be proud of the worthy combat that ultimately provided the trophy he would now go home and sacrifice.

He was anxious to get back to China and offer up the thumb at the family altar, then handsomely reward his source who provided the information that made it so easy. There had been only one black insurance agent in town, and just as the information indicated, he drove a Mercedes and was probably about the right age, although Phun really had no idea how old Cruiser was.

He had been thrown by his sister's presence, though, and wondered if he should have known she'd be there. He prided himself on predicting what people would do, and anticipating who might show up for any particular fight. Yet nothing had clued him about her, and her presence could have been a fatal distraction if he hadn't been so focused on killing Cruiser, or if Cruiser had been a better challenge.

Phun packed the few things he had but kept the knife separate so he could toss it out the window on his drive back to Charlotte. He didn't want to deal with checking out of the motel, but he rather liked the friendly old woman who ran the front desk. Age was to be respected, and so to walk out without generously thanking her for her hospitality would show her the same contempt that Americans seemed to feel toward old people. He was Chinese, and therefore better.

The old woman smiled and touched his hand and told him what weather to expect in Charlotte as she tilted her head to see through her bifocals, up or down depending on whether she was looking at him or his thick wad of money. She gave him a receipt and then handed him a large envelope with his name written in Mandarin.

"A kid on a bicycle dropped it off an hour ago," she said. "He said it was for one of my guests. I don't recognize the name but I thought it might be for you since that looks like Chinese writing to me and you, well, look more Chinese than the family in room six or the fisherman in two."

He stopped on the small porch and opened it, shocked that anyone knew he was there and completely unable to guess what they might want to give him.

Inside the envelope were photos of his dead family, as heartbreaking and tormenting as anything in this life could ever be. Accompanying them was a note that apologized deeply for their deaths. It also ridiculed him for thinking Cruiser could ever be easy to kill, and promised that Phun would never see China again.

Phun stared at the note, controlling his breathing so his anger would not run away with him. He folded it neatly and put it back in the envelope. As he walked to his rental car he stopped and gently petted the old lady's dog. Then he fed it the thumb of last night's mistake.

5

Jennifer had dreamed for years of the moment she would see her brother again. She'd spent much of that time training to kill him. So as she sat in her car after her walk from the bar she tried to tighten her focus on that dream, while fighting her confusion over why she didn't tell her boss she'd watched Phun kill Lenny last night.

Lenny had taken her to the boat ramp to show her the bats feeding in the moonlight, and Phun had come powerfully out of nowhere, so quick and ruthless that it stunned even her, pinning her feet to the ground as Phun slashed and brutalized him. Twice Phun looked to make sure she wasn't going to attack, and once, when she did step close, he grabbed her neck and threw her down so hard it knocked her breathless.

There was no way she could have told her boss any of that. Her admiration for Phun's skill and power might have leaked out, probably in quiet tones of fear that her boss might have misinterpreted as love for a brutal brother who tore Lenny apart in just a few seconds.

Phun walked over to her afterward, rotating Lenny's thumb between his fingers and examining it with satisfaction before jamming it into his pocket. He stood over her like a wild and unpredictable animal, but even with the insanity and savagery of his actions still boring through his black eyes, she doubted he would hurt her.

As he eased away from attack he switched hands with his knife and dug into his other pocket to pull out two pieces of candy. He tossed one her way, then un-wrapped the other and popped it playfully into his mouth. "Remember these?"

She looked at the candy as if it were nothing special.

"I haven't had them for years," he said. "They sell them here."

She said nothing as he chewed noisily and savored the taste. Then he licked his lips and walked into the darkness.

A minute passed before Jennifer moved at all. It was no longer fear that kept her on the ground, but disgust over what Phun had done, and shame for not doing what she'd trained so long to do. Her chance had come and gone and she'd done nothing, so not only was Phun still alive, now he also knew she was afraid of him.

No one back at MI6 had suggested a contingency plan for the unlikely scenario that she found Phun before she found Cruiser, but it was clear she no longer needed to seek Cruiser as an ally. She could go right to her mission to kill her brother, at least as soon as she wiggled out of the town's limelight enough to work in the shadows.

A woman walked past her parked car and stared with her eyes accusing Jennifer of killing Lenny. Jennifer needed to look innocent and so she waved pleasantly, but the woman flicked her cigarette in Jennifer's direction and kept going to a small playground next to the parking lot.

Jennifer watched the beautiful little children swing in the cool evening air while their mothers eyed her with suspicion. She respected them for wanting to protect their kids, even though she would quite willingly give up her life to protect any child and therefore could never be a threat to them.

She hoped she would be a good mother if she ever got the chance, but that seemed less and less likely with each month that passed. Like so many women before her, she found herself racing at an uncontrollable speed through the intersection of Family and Career, where not making a conscious decision to have a family yielded the exact same results as deciding against it. The intensity of her career demanded that work be her primary road, and it offered few exits to the secondary roads on which she suspected she might find happiness.

Even though they probably couldn't see through the glare of her windshield, she smiled at the women and felt the tiniest bit of kinship because Buxton really was the kind of town where she could be comfortable. The cool evening breezes, broad open porches and respect for the ocean reminded her of the home in Selsey she vacationed whenever she had a chance. The pretense of buying a house from Stewart had shaken loose her hope to settle down, and Buxton had a nice feeling of community to it, something she knew she would prize after so much time alone and in motion.

So there it suddenly was – a plan that came from emotions and not intellect, a decision to finish this mission and then make a drastic change, paying the expensive toll to start down a new road that she hoped would provide more happiness than the one on which she now traveled. She would waste no more time trying to find Cruiser, even though it would have been exciting to meet the legendary man who was idolized in the spy trade.

She could kill Phun and finish this, *all* of this, and be done. That made her excited in a way she barely remembered ever feeling before. Phun was close by and reachable while trying to avenge the deaths of a wife and children Jennifer had never met and didn't care about. Even though they were her family, they were also her enemies because of their relationship with Phun. Besides, he deserved the pain of their deaths, almost as much as he deserved the pain of his own.

Ironically, her boss had doubted her convictions to kill Phun. Maybe he'd been right after all, but at the time he would never have questioned her resolve if he could have just looked into her soul and seen the passion that burned there to kill him.

There was a time, though, back when she was fifteen and innocent, that she'd almost joined him.

"Why do you follow his rules?" Phun asked as she joined him in the garden of their home.

"Why don't you? He's our father."

"You'd think he was the father of China, the way he tries to change it to suit his vision."

"He uses his influence in ways he thinks best for all Chinese. It's noble of him."

"You just can't see the consequences if he succeeds."

"You've told me many times. You could be right, I'm not sure."

"I am right, and someone needs to stop him before he fills everybody's heads with his ideas."

She laughed. "And *you're* going to do it? You're lucky he still lets you live here. He told Mother that if you get in trouble again he'll tell his men not to let you return."

"He is the one who is lucky. I have my own men. If I had his money I wouldn't let him live here or anywhere."

"Those criminals you run with?"

"We're radicals. Not criminals. Be careful with your words."

"Some of them are murderers. Father told me."

"*Most* of us are murderers."

At that she walked away.

That same night he came home bloody and filled with the taste of slaughter.

"Father," he yelled, loud enough for his voice to resonate through the family mansion.

Jennifer jumped out of bed and ran down the hall as their father came out of his study. When he did, Phun stabbed him dozens of times in the chest.

"You will not destroy the China of my future" Phun shouted as Jennifer cried and her mother pulled him off of her husband's dying body.

Fear of Phun kept Jennifer and her mother obedient for more than a year after that. Phun ran the house and set the rules under which they lived until they managed to escape through the British Embassy.

And so Jennifer, too, was in North Carolina to avenge a murder. She'd had doubts last night about whether or not she could do it, surprised by an instinctual devotion to family. But both were gone this morning as she shivered with the realization of how closely his attack on Lenny resembled his attack on their father.

She would use her father's brutal murder to block her good memories of playing tag with Phun in the family temple, but she would have to be vigilant about it, especially since killing wasn't something she liked to do. She'd killed enough to know that even with orders and facts she believed, it was always ugly and emotionally hard. She'd turned down two assignments that couldn't support the weight of her conscience because she always needed to believe that society, however broad or narrow that definition was applied, would be better off for the death. If it was nothing more than a wash, she wouldn't do the job.

Even now, her hatred of Phun for killing their father wasn't quite enough. But he was orchestrating war, buying weapons that would indiscriminately kill millions of people in the United States and England.

It was dusk when she finally decided to leave the Hatteras Realty parking lot. As soon as she turned the key, Sheriff Phillips pulled up and leaned out his window. He didn't speak and she didn't either, so after twenty seconds she pulled away and waited for a break in the traffic before pulling out onto the main road. Phillips followed and then turned on his lights and siren. She pulled over and he stopped behind her, leaving his lights flashing as he got out.

"License and registration, please."

"Mind telling me what I did?"

"There was no left turn allowed back there."

"There wasn't a sign."

"It's all right, ma'am. I'm just giving you a warning."

"Can't tell you how relieved I am. Something like that on my record would devastate me."

"You've got kind of a smart mouth, don't you, ma'am?"

"I'm smart, period. Does that intimidate you?"

"To be honest, I'm a little fascinated with you."

"Sorry to say that I'd find it impossible to reciprocate. Will this take long?"

Cars slowed as they passed, the drivers taking a good look to see who their sheriff was interrogating, slowing down even more once they realized it was Jennifer.

"Just one thing more, ma'am. Mind stepping out of the car?"

"You've got to be kidding."

"No ma'am. Keep your hands where I can see them as you step out."

She smiled and stared but didn't move an inch.

"I told you –"

"To keep my hands where you could see them and step out of the car. What I'm trying to decide is how to open my door while keeping my hands where you can see them."

Phillips looked embarrassed for a second, then opened her door.

"Thank you."

"Step in front of your vehicle. In the headlights where I can watch you. Mind if I look inside your vehicle?"

"Look or search? You're already looking, so I'm guessing you want to search, and if I understand your laws correctly you don't have the right."

"You might be right, which is why I asked. But if I don't get to *look* I'm going to arrest you for assaulting Joe in the bar. Remember him?" He jabbed his thumb back toward his car where Joe sat watching. "Little drunk guy with a slow-moving finger."

"Oh, I see. Well then by all means you should search my car."

"Just a cursory one," he said as he pulled on latex gloves.

"While I stand here in the headlights becoming even more of a suspect to the people driving by." She waved at a car slowing down, confusing the occupants who slowly raised their hands and, with stupid looks on their faces, waved back.

"You're a clever woman." He clicked on her high beams, making it impossible to see what he was doing.

A minute later he said, "Thanks for your cooperation. Be careful of traffic as you come around the side."

"I bet I'm going to see you tomorrow, Sheriff."

"Hurricane, you know. I'll be busy evacuating people."

She saw Phillips watching as she idled a few feet, then spun her tires and threw gravel at him and his car. She stopped and leaned out the window. "I'm so sorry. Not used to these powerful American cars, I'm afraid."

*   *   *

Phillips was proud of himself for being so clever with the knife he'd smeared with Lenny and Joe's blood. While pretending to rifle through the English woman's glove box, he'd reached low and behind the passenger seat and stuck the tip of the knife through the leather seam, pushing the entire blade and handle inside the seat until it was unnoticeable along the inside edge.

Then he and Joe followed her back to the little motel where she was staying, a two-story rectangle of concrete block with a flat roof and handrails rusting from the salt air. After he parked he asked Joe to pour two more beers into cups.

"I ain't bothered about my finger, Trent, so what are we doing watching her? We need to be doing something about Ernie Roberts."

"I'm thinking, Joe, and enjoying the night. It really is beautiful here."

"I liked it better before Lenny got himself killed."

"I told you not to worry. I won't let Roberts get you. Do you think she's in for the night?"

"Who cares?"

Just then she stepped in front of the window long enough to close the drapes. Five minutes later the lights went out.

Phillips moved the car so it would look like he'd left, then reparked and opened the last of the beers. He felt fairly confident she wasn't going out again because it was almost eleven and there really wasn't much to do in a small town bracing for bad weather. He'd also drunk enough beer to do the awful but necessary thing to Joe.

Traffic was light when he pulled out on the road, listening to Joe whine about leaving Buxton and wondering what he could get for his house, saying there was nothing to keep him from putting his house on the market and getting out of town as soon as it survived the hurricane.

"Hey Joe, let's go north and have a few drinks? We haven't been to that place you like in Kill Devil Hills for months."

"Not really in the mood, and besides, the waitress who used to treat me nice moved away. And I need a shave before I go out where women are."

"You want to sit around here and worry? Go home and watch television and wait for Roberts to slice you up?" Phillips flicked an imaginary knife at Joe's face and made him jump.

"You think that's funny?"

"Kind of."

Joe was such a nice guy that it made him an easy target for a joke. Phillips sure didn't want to kill him, and so he searched for options, keeping Maggie's idea as a last resort kind of thing.

"Joe, I was thinking about Ernie Roberts."

"You think I'm sitting here pondering my phone bill?"

"If we find him, we could end this."

"Do you have enough reason to arrest him?"

"I'm not talking about arrest."

"Then what…what are you thinking, Trent?"

"Probably same as you. We could eliminate this risk without exposing ourselves. But you'd have to swear to keep your mouth shut about it, and about our past."

Joe turned in his seat so his back was against the door. "You talking about killing him? I want no part of that."

"Me, neither, but we didn't ask Roberts to come back here and threaten us. We're only defending ourselves. You know as well as me that he's come here to kill us."

"Maybe, but I'm no murderer. He comes into my house and attacks me I'll figure I've got good reason to defend myself. Until then, doing what you say makes me as bad as him. Worse, maybe."

"Come on, Joe, what if he does kill you? Who'll take care of your mother? You know I'll try, but I've got a lot of ground to cover. Besides, Roberts might even get me before you."

"Then I'll have to trust that Momma can take care of herself 'cause I ain't no murderer and never have been. You done painted me with your violence once. You're not doing it again."

Phillips started to argue, but there wasn't any point and he knew it. For all of Joe's weaknesses, when he took a firm position it never changed.

"Come on then, we're going to some bars in Nag's Head. I've got a change of clothes in back. We'll get your car and ride."

"I guess. But no more talk about murder."

"No more talk," said Phillips, and he meant it.

Ten minutes later they pulled up to Joe's house. Phillips stayed at the car and changed into some old clothes, then grabbed the second fillet knife he'd bought in Ocracoke. It was exactly like the one smeared with Joe and Lenny's blood and then planted in Jennifer's Expedition.

He went inside and waited until Joe came out of his bedroom dressed nicely, and wearing the fancy cologne he saved for special occasions. He stared at Phillips's old clothes.

"You're going out dressed like that, Trent?"

Phillips didn't answer. He was concentrating much too hard on what he had to do.

6

It had been a long day of patience for Jay Stewart. He'd sat around his office until five waiting for Jennifer to show up, and then had no choice but to hang around the bar long after she broke Joe's finger.

The bartender ignored him, making it clear that he hoped he would leave. So Stewart nursed his beer for more than an hour and waited for someone else to walk over and help out with his plans. Finally two guys from the boatyard came over and one of them bought a round.

"What's the deal with the babe from England?" asked the thin guy wearing an Evinrude t-shirt.

"Don't know much about her," Stewart said. "Just met her yesterday. Trying to sell her a house."

"Great looking lady," said the other.

"At the very least, she is that." Stewart lifted his beer and they clinked bottles. "You guys hear what they said about her and Lenny?"

"I can't imagine her as a killer."

Evinrude chuckled. "All women are killers. Most just do it slower and stretch it out over a lifetime."

"He's been divorced three times," the other man said.

"And every one of them divorces was worth the cost. You were with her right before Lenny?"

"That's right. We were having a pleasant dinner when Lenny walked over. They seemed to know each other and were polite enough, but acted a little like two enemies forced to make nice in public."

"No shit. You tell that to the sheriff?"

"I tried at breakfast but he cut me off. So screw him, you know."

"Phillips is a blunt fella and hard to get sometimes. Want me to pass it on to him?"

"Tell whoever you like. Means nothing to me. Doubt she'll buy a home here now so I already lost my commission."

"I'll make sure he knows," he said excitedly as he headed off to talk to the sheriff's deputy.

Stewart had to maintain distance from Jennifer now that he'd provided more evidence that she killed Lenny, but there was another reason to keep his distance that played more powerfully into his actions than he wanted to admit.

The truth was she'd somehow jogged lose that painful memory of what he'd lost in Simone, and he could not allow it to become a weakness. Maybe after Phun was dead and he could move on with his life, but not now.

When he left the bar he'd passed Jennifer standing on the shoulder of the road in the blinding light of her own high beams, the wind snapping at her clothes while Phillips searched her car and Joe looked on from the patrol car. Stewart drove another mile and then doubled back, but the sheriff had already let her go.

So he followed the sheriff at a distance to Jennifer's motel and waited for them to leave, just a little unsure of what to do next because Lenny's brutal murder and the bruise on Jennifer's neck confirmed that Phun was in town. He might try to hurt or kill Jennifer, and Stewart wanted to protect her because he needed her help.

His well-honed instincts screamed "liar", so maybe she really *was* starting to mean something to him. Or were the feelings just old ones for Simone that he'd rediscovered, like a comfortable sweater packed away in the back of a drawer.

He'd learned in China that Phun had a sister who was a Royal Marine sharpshooter. It was a riddle of Phun's that "The blood of the blood I shed wants mine, for that blood is my own."

It was easy for Cruiser to find her after that, but she disappeared into the Secret Intelligence Service before he found out what her brother looked like. When a Chinese-speaking sharpshooter female applied to partner up with his replacement in China, his opportunity created itself.

The first time they met he instantly knew why he'd failed to find Phun. He'd wasted his time chasing Phun under an assumption that a Chinese radical would look Chinese, but Jennifer proved the error. It was his own trick played back on him, the same way he'd made everyone believe that Cruiser was black.

Her looks no longer bothered him, but the fact that he liked her put his insides in knots. It was weird to feel good about someone whose brother had sworn to slice off his face, and he wrestled with those feelings, separating brother from sister and friend from enemy until finally deciding to isolate his feelings the same way Phun had done all those years ago. Phun hated his father but loved his mother and sister enough to let them escape China. He could have stopped them from leaving, but inside Phun's vicious soul was a man who cared for Jennifer in opposition to the hatred he unleashed on their father. If Phun could balance those feelings, Stewart could too.

But could Jennifer? It wasn't completely impossible that Stewart might win a fight with Phun, and if he did, how would that sit with her? If she cared for either of them, what price would he pay for killing her brother? Less than if he lost, of course, but more than if he didn't fight Phun at all.

He was confused, which rarely happened, so when Phillips left Jennifer's motel, he followed, even though Phun was most likely nearby, close to the sister he hadn't seen in twenty years, maybe staying a room or two away and careful not to be seen.

Phillips' patrol car turned into Joe's driveway. Stewart drove past as Phillips disappeared against the solid dark backdrop of water in the distance. He pulled into a vacant lot two blocks away, grabbed his small pack, and then trotted carefully from tree to tree along the drive. The porch light was on at a small cottage, two hundred feet away from Phillips's car, and even though the cottage was dark inside, he avoided it anyway.

He sneaked onto the porch of the main house and looked through the open windows. The house was tidy inside, verging on prissy, with an afghan over the back of the couch and a large collection of crystal figurines in a glass case and on the fireplace mantle.

Stewart pulled out his camera, and with the wind covering the noise he clicked pictures as Joe stared at the clothes Sheriff Phillips was wearing and asked, "You're going out dressed like that, Trent?"

The sheriff didn't answer. He took a menacing step toward Joe and then stopped, surveying the room like a photographer seeking the best lighting.

"What's going on, Trent?"

The contrast of size between Phillips and Joe was almost comedic. Joe moved away as Phillips stepped toward him with deep reluctance in his eyes. Stewart could guess they were about to fight but he couldn't believe it, and it didn't look like either of them could either as Phillips moved toward Joe in slow steps. When Joe backed up against the wall, Phillips stepped closer and put his big hand to Joe's neck.

"I'm sorry, Joe. I promised not to let Roberts get you, and I promised Maggie you wouldn't talk to the state police. Only way I know to do both."

But then Phillips dropped his eyes and let go.

Joe took a step sideways and Phillips didn't stop him. He took another step, and then turned and ran. He cracked open the front door and was just about to get away when Phillips leaped over the sofa and slammed the door shut. He pinned Joe against the wall with his left hand, his arm stretched out with muscles bulging.

Joe hit him in the stomach, his small hands hammering away to no effect. He stomped on Phillips's feet and tried to push him away but nothing worked or seemed to upset Phillips. He just let Joe hit him as if waiting for his own temper to rise. Joe kept hitting and struggling but Phillips just stood there, not letting him escape but not hurting him either.

"Be a man about this, Joe."

"You done this once, Trent, and now you're here 'cause of that. Don't screw up twice. Let it go and we'll have those drinks. Maybe meet me a nice woman."

"Don't make this harder than it already is."

"Sorry, but didn't know I was to worry about you."

Phillips smiled. Then he let go and took a step back. He laughed, turning his back to Joe and laughing in the relieved kind of way that runs seconds ahead or closely behind an ugly task. Stewart ducked when Phillips's eyes passed over his window, and when he raised back up Joe was laughing too, as though this was a game they played all the time.

Then Phillips slashed off most of Joe's nose.

"Damn," Phillips said. "Don't move like that."

Joe didn't move again. He didn't even touch to see if his nose was really gone. He seemed in shock as he stared at Phillips, who threw him onto the floor and went for his face, but then Joe came to life and wriggled around like a kid refusing medicine, planting his feet and sliding forward and dragging Phillips along the floor.

As Stewart watched from outside the house, his fear of Phun swelled almost out of control because all of Phun's victims had been alive when he'd skinned their faces, yet he'd done it with near-surgical precision. Yet here was big, muscular, Trent Phillips being forced to make wild slashes at a man as small as Joe. God, what kind of man was Phun to make it so easy? Lenny had been twice Joe's size, yet the newspaper had noted the careful precision with which he'd been tortured.

Joe kept sliding and wiggling and kicking and screaming as Phillips held him down and slashed at his face, trying to emulate Phun but doing a poor job of it, slicing off pieces of his ear and lacerating the flesh instead of removing it completely.

Phillips jammed his knee into Joe's stomach to shut him up, and as Joe struggled for air Phillips put the knife to Joe's left cheek and sliced down to his jaw. Joe screamed but Phillips seemed possessed. He didn't close his eyes or turn away as he pulled the meat away from one check and then the other.

Joe stopped moving and Stewart guessed he'd passed out. Phillips stood up, grabbed Joe's hand and tried to pull off his thumb. He couldn't do it. He tried again, wiping Joe's slippery blood onto his old trousers so he could get a better grip. After several attempts he let the hand fall to the floor and walked through the kitchen to the garage.

Stewart slid down and hid until Phillips came back and passed his window. When he looked again, Joe was gone. Phillips was alone in the small living room.

"What the hell?" Phillips said, and just as he did Joe charged in from the bedroom, his face missing but his machete back and ready to slice into Phillips. Stewart clicked more photos as Joe took a swing at Phillips, who grabbed his wrist and stopped it.

The machete fell and clanged onto the floor as the momentum carried both of them toward Stewart's window. They crashed into it and almost came through the screen, and as they did, Stewart saw Joe look out and see him.

It was a horrible sight as Joe's panicked eyes looked down from his bloody face, but once he saw Stewart he seemed to give up. He stopped fighting and fell away from Phillips, who smashed his fist into the flat remains of his nose.

Joe went down and Phillips grabbed his hand in a panic that seemed nearly insane, clamped onto his thumb with pliers and after several tries ripped it off. Then he slid the knife deep into both of Joe's ears, looked quickly around the house, and left.

Stewart didn't move for a long time. He sat on the porch and leaned against the wall, trying to think like a professional but having a rough time after seeing the hideous way he would die if he fought Phun and lost.

He pushed his mind around that worry by forcing a decision about whether or not to plant evidence to make it obvious Phillips had killed Joe. But it would be pointless. Sheriff Phillips would be in charge of the investigation and would discard whatever Stewart left anyway.

Stewart had some guesses about why Phillips wanted Joe dead, but the reason didn't matter. He would weave the murder into his plans to divert attention away from him when Phun finally died.

7

Jennifer couldn't sleep and had sat for hours struggling with thoughts that only surfaced when she was either making mistakes or confused. She would have liked to talk them over with her mother, whose decisions she'd trusted completely when they'd escaped Phun – leaving behind their elite life and family fortune and starting over with absolutely nothing in England. But since getting the assignment to kill Phun Jennifer had avoided her because although her mother hated what Phun had done, he was still her son and she loved him. She would never understand Jennifer's lust to kill him.

So she would get by without her, just as she'd gotten by without men for so long, and as she sat on the bed feeling stupid for making two amateurish mistakes in two days, Nigel chimed in to make her feel even worse.

An older man with enormous self-confidence who filtered his power through gentleness, Nigel had been one of her early supervisors. His strengths gave her the same sense of safety she'd had until her father died, so she amazed herself by trusting him with the power to protect her, knowing full well that it also gave him the power to hurt her.

Looking back she could see that she'd needed to expose herself to him, if for no other reason than to prove that her hatred of Phun hadn't killed her ability to love a man, or the faith and willingness to take risks for a relationship. At one point she even thought about leaving the Service to raise their family, but she never had to make that decision because toward the end of their second year together, Nigel started seeing a woman who worked in the documents section at Thames House.

Jennifer was just about the last person to find out, so not only did she feel stupid and humiliated, she also looked professionally incompetent. How could she be expected to spy successfully on foreign nations when she wasn't even aware of her lover's affair?

She vowed to never again open herself to that kind of pain and humiliation, and from that point would forever keep her goals and dreams private, known only to herself. She would hide her fears and insecurities the same way. She'd done with Nigel what she set out to do and proven she was willing to love and trust a man, so men were the problem, not her.

Although she would always miss the great feeling of being in love, she wouldn't miss the pain, especially since Nigel's cheating was still a laugh back at headquarters. She would never be a joke again, but she had slipped a little with the estate agent, Jay Stewart. Although he hadn't bought it, she actually meant a little of the way she acted toward him. Stroking his hand when he'd shown up for breakfast was genuine; she was glad to see him.

It didn't matter, though, because he clearly wasn't interested in her. He'd proven that by putting her under the sheriff's suspicion. But even so, it was nice to know she was still capable of the feeling that brought with it some hope for the dream she'd found necessary to abandon, a life far different than the one for which she was braced and ready to live.

She liked the way Stewart seemed to have insight into her that he could use as a weapon, but that he didn't feel like a threat. If the stakes weren't so incredibly high, whatever game he was playing actually could have been nice, almost intimate.

She sat on her bed and fantasized about things that could never be part of her future. As always, that made her sad about the life she'd chosen. She liked to think that someday she would walk away from it and have a normal relationship with someone secure enough to accept her. But she knew the odds. After years in a career of playing people, and making sure no one played her, she would be far too jaded and hard for anyone normal. That would leave her completely alone for the rest of her life, except for a mother she no longer saw and a murderous brother she wanted dead.

Not only did she want Phun dead, she'd always wanted to be the one to kill him. But she was even confused about that now, looking for the first time through her mother's eyes at a confused young man who'd wound up in trouble. All the venom she'd stored up for years had been diluted by the discovery that she still had at least a little room in her heart for Phun. No matter how much she wished it wasn't true, she didn't really want him to die, at least by her hand.

It was a confusing mix of emotions because she also had a job to do and orders to kill him. She had pushed hard for the chance, and was one of the few people in the world who could actually do it. She could get close to Phun, and that elite position made it critical that she focus on what he'd done to her father, and the plans he had to make England suffer.

The poison-filled freighter that sunk in the Pacific was just a calling card into the world of terrorism. His money and determination had already gained him access to the leaders of terrorist groups from the Philippines to Saudi Arabia, and his intelligence, education, and non-Muslim background were assets everyone wanted to use to the fullest advantage. He'd strengthened any area where his organization might have fallen short, and he now lacked nothing. He had to be stopped, and she knew what he looked like, the friends he'd built allegiances with when he was young and just rising to power, their interests, and the places they probably still gathered in secret. All of that enabled her to ambush and kill Phun.

She went back to bed and tried to sleep, but the air conditioner rattled and the couple next door partied late. The night passed slowly until she was shocked out of a half-consciousness by a pounding on her door. She pulled on a robe and ran a hand through her hair, eased the drapes aside and saw Sheriff Phillips standing outside with his deputy, who'd pulled his cap down ridiculously low to keep the wind from blowing it off. The sun was up so she must have slept after all, although she sure didn't feel like it.

She opened the door and the deputy stepped back. He had his pistol out, but kept it pointed at the ground as if he'd never really aimed at anyone before. The hammer was down but the safety was off. She thought about snatching it out of his hand just to scare him.

"Thought you might still be asleep, ma'am," Phillips said as he leaned against the rail of the balcony with his arms folded across his chest. "Since you had yourself such a late night."

She did not allow her confusion to show as she stepped out of her room while the deputy craned to see who might be inside. She blocked his view with her body, just to keep him wondering.

"You're the one who looks tired, Sheriff. Or scared. For the life of me I can't tell which."

Phillips acted like he'd been caught out of character. He straightened up and hardened the look on his face as his deputy turned to him and said, "She's right, Sheriff, you do —"

"Shut up."

"It looks to me like you and your little friend might have spent the night in my parking lot. In which case, Sheriff, you certainly must know that I never left my room."

Phillips didn't speak as if choosing his words carefully. The deputy waited. Despite her determination not to do it, she clutched her robe and closed it more tightly.

"Partly true," he finally said, as he continued to look her over. "But we...I...went home after you turned off your lights. So I have no idea what you did later. You must feel pretty important to think I'd hang around here watching your window when I've got a doozie of a storm blowing this way."

"I see," she said. "Mind answering a question for me then, Chief?"

"Sheriff."

"Right."

"I'll try. I'm just a country boy, you know. Don't expect too much."

"I don't."

"Your question?"

"If you have no idea what I did, why are you here on such a busy day with guns drawn as if I'm under arrest? You must have some idea I broke a law to justify your presence, so which is it? No idea or some idea?"

"Who said anything about you being under arrest?"

"This is ridiculous. Go back to checking fishing licenses." She half-turned toward her room but then lurched forward to spook the deputy. "Boo!"

He jumped back into the railing and almost dropped his gun. Jennifer laughed and so did the sheriff, both of them pointing at the deputy. They were still laughing when she asked, "I am under arrest, aren't I?"

"No," he wiped his eyes. "God, that was funny."

"Big joke," said the deputy. "Ha, ha."

"Damn funny. Anyway, ma'am, I just need to ask you some questions, that's all."

"Do I have a choice?"

"No ma'am."

"Then give me five minutes to get dressed." She backed into her room, but the sheriff followed and then closed the door.

"Sorry ma'am. You might have been involved in a murder, so I can't very well let you out of my sight. How would it look if you got away through a back door or window?"

She waved her arm around the room. "Well there isn't a back door or another window, so…what? You're going to sit there while I dress?"

He sat on the bed and bounced a little. "Don't see as I have much choice."

"You could turn your back and pretend to be a gentleman."

"I could but I won't."

111

"Very nice. Why doesn't that surprise me?"

"I don't get the impression that very much surprises you. Least of all me."

"You're being too honest with yourself."

She picked some panties out of her suitcase, and with her back to him she slipped them on under her robe. She pulled up her jeans, put a shirt over her back before dropping her robe, snapped on a bra, and then threaded her arms through the straps and shirtsleeves. She turned around and glared at him as she buttoned her shirt. "Enjoy that?"

He took a deep breath and stood up. "Let's go. I don't need to cuff you."

"Jesus, then I'm not really much of a murder suspect, am I?"

The deputy was grinning as they stepped out, but he stopped when he saw Phillips's face. As they went down the steps to the parking lot, Phillips got a call on his cell phone. After checking the number he answered it and said "Hold on." Then he walked off a good distance, even though the wind was strong enough to keep anyone from overhearing. He came back looking angry and confused.

"Okay, ma'am, seems like there's been a break in the case. Maybe I was wrong about you. Think that's possible?"

"I wouldn't have to think about it. I would know whether or not I killed someone, Chief."

"Sher...I should still ask you some questions. Would you follow me down to my office? Just take an hour or so."

"You want me to come now, I suppose."

"Yes, *now*. Lady, is anything easy with you?"

She stared at her car keys in the deputy's hand. "Good-byes are," she said as she snatched her keys. "Good-bye."

She expected the deputy to try to stop her, and he did, which made her laugh because he didn't have any idea what he was dealing with as he grabbed her by the arm. She could have twisted him like a pretzel, broken his neck, grabbed his pistol and then killed both him and the sheriff in less time than it took to sneeze.

But she just stood there and waited until Phillips told him to let her go, then went to her car and started it. She pulled over to where the two men stood. "Coming?" she asked, and then drove out of the parking lot toward town.

*   *   *

Phillips suddenly felt like shit, standing in the motel parking lot realizing that neither he nor Joe had ever been in any danger from Ernie Roberts.

After Lenny was murdered, Phillips had filed a *Request for Recent Contact* on Roberts through the FBI, and the caller just told him that Roberts had been in a Richmond jail for seventeen weeks, and would remain there several more months until the verdict in his trial on drug charges.

It hardly mattered who else might have killed Lenny because there was nothing personal about it, expect perhaps between Lenny and the man who murdered him. Why in God's name had he shot off his mouth to Maggie?

She'd had a hot bath and a tall drink ready when he got home from Joe's house.

"How did it go, Trent?"

"It was terrible."

"Tell me about it."

"No."

"*Trent.*"

He climbed into the tub and didn't speak as he scrubbed his hands while she washed his back.

"Did he say anything unexpected?"

113

He closed his eyes and took a drink.

"Did he cry?"

She washed his legs up to his crotch. He took a long drink. She slipped off her robe and put a foot into the tub.

"Go to bed, Maggie."

She looked embarrassed and offended. "I'm trying to –"

"Just do me a favor and go to bed."

If he'd never told her, his past would still be a secret and Joe would still be alive. But if Joe hadn't wanted to call the state police, he would still be alive anyway, so his death was really his own fault.

The only trouble now was the plan he'd built around three deaths and a serial killer. He'd gone to Jennifer's motel planning to arrest her for Lenny's murder based upon the knife he would find in her car. After that, he could easily build a case for her killing Joe, especially since both murders were done the same way and she was already connected to both victims.

As Jennifer disappeared down the road toward town he believed the plan could still work, perhaps even better if he made a big show of her arrest? A lot of witnesses would go a long way toward convicting her of killing Lenny, at least in the public's opinion. As news of last night's murder leaked out, the townspeople would automatically assume she'd also killed Joe, the great guy with bad timing. All his life, whether asking out a girl or telling a joke, Joe's timing had been horrible, but it had never been worse than last night, dying only a few hours before Phillips got the call from the FBI.

In the light of day he could barely believe he'd tortured and killed his best friend. But he *had* done it, so he still had to act like he was dealing with exactly the same problem he'd had before – a serial killer appeared to be carving up

114

residents of Buxton. Someone had to be caught, and it was Phillips's job to do the catching.

Phillips had only been toying with the English woman until now, building a case against her so he could dazzle the townsfolk when he killed Roberts, the *real* murderer, and proving once again how much smarter he was than the people he protected. He would impress them with his ability to see beyond their own simple assumptions that Jennifer was guilty, and that brilliance would keep him in office for the rest of his life.

That idea vanished the instant he learned Roberts couldn't have killed Lenny, and that gave him no choice but to arrest her and get her convicted of both murders, heading off any questions into what he'd done to Joe.

He pulled out of the motel parking lot, deciding to search her car at a very public place where nosy onlookers would gawk like they always did. He would pull the razor-sharp fillet knife with Lenny and Joe's blood from the fold of her passenger seat. It would be damned compelling evidence and brilliant police work.

He would make it look hard, of course, letting his deputy drag her to his car while he pulled out the trunk liner and carpet and cut open the seats – things he wouldn't normally do but could get away with once he produced the knife. Probable cause could be almost anything. Hell, he'd say she confessed in the motel room if he had to. His word against hers.

When Jennifer was right in front of Wal-Mart he raced around her car and slammed on his brakes, siren wailing and lights flashing as he slid sideways to a stop. Phillips jumped out and ducked behind his front fender while the deputy scooted around the rear. They both aimed their guns through her windshield while Phillips gave the orders.

"Hands on the wheel. Keep 'em where I can see them."

She didn't move as Phillips waited for a crowd to assemble. It only took a minute for Wal-Mart to empty as though it was on fire. Phillips heard people talking, but he didn't look away as he stood up with his gun trained on Jennifer. He walked toward the car without blinking. "Out of the car!"

He flung open the door, pulled her out, and threw her against the side of her Expedition. He searched her and the deputy put on cuffs, then hustled her to the side of Phillips's car as the crowd moved ever closer.

"Stay back, folks. She's a suspect in two murders. I've been investigating her involvement in Lenny's death, and now that Joe's dead –" He stopped and looked like he'd slipped up.

Someone said "Joe's dead?" and everyone repeated it like a secret shared quickly.

"I shouldn't have said that. Figured word was already out."

He dug around in the trunk, glancing up from time to time to look at the crowd and, just as he hoped, saw every one looking like they despised Jennifer. At one point he leaned out of her car and shouted "Deputy, you shoot her if she moves."

Then he ceremoniously pulled the knife out of Jennifer's car and held it up while the crowd gasped. The deputy looked shocked before taking dead aim and shouting "Get down on the ground lady!"

Phillips heard her stammering as she went to her knees. She stayed there while the deputy and everyone else seemed to ponder how to get her into the car from a kneeling position.

"Don't you dare move while I check those handcuffs," the deputy said as he performed a save-face check of the lock. Then he helped her up and stuffed her into the back of the sheriff's car. The crowd cheered and the manager of Wal-Mart walked over to congratulate his amazing sheriff.

"It's just evidence," Phillips said. "Doesn't necessarily mean she killed Lenny. Or Joe for that matter."

"Of course not," the manager laughed. "I hide bloody knives in my car all the time."

8

Phillips told the deputy to wait for the tow truck, and then he drove away with Jennifer. He wanted to know how strongly she suspected him of murdering Joe, since she knew damned well she hadn't done it.

"You said last night that you understand our laws a little. Know Miranda?"

She stayed silent.

"If you want to say anything, I'll use it against you. That is unless you can explain away the knife."

She leaned forward so she could whisper through the holes of the Plexiglas. "I think explaining away the knife will be your job. You must be the one who hid it there. I bet I can prove it."

"Yeah, yeah, everyone who commits a crime is innocent. Guess it was foolish to think you'd act different."

"*You're* not."

"Different?"

"Innocent. I bet you killed Joe, if in fact he is dead. You were with him last night when you stopped me and I bet there are lots of other people who saw you together. But you don't have any idea who killed Lenny, or what you're up against. That's kind of funny to me."

"I've got a pretty good hunch that Lenny's blood is on that knife. It might be hard to prove you did it, though. You're pretty smart. I haven't underrated your intelligence. In fact, I've already admitted to being fascinated with you."

"You're a bit clumsy to reach so far. Intellectually, I mean. You're married?"

"More'n twenty years."

"I bet your wife didn't finish high school."

"Leave Maggie out … Boston College." He had no idea where the name came from.

"Then I can't imagine what you two find to talk about."

"Don't pretend to know me, lady. Don't think I'm merely the strong arm of the law and nothing else."

"You flatter yourself."

"God, you really are a bitch."

"You set me up as a murderer. We'll see how nice you are after I turn that table around."

"With a wild imagination."

"It's obvious to everyone that I scare you."

"You scare me?"

"Still, I bet you fuck Maggie with me on your mind."

"Shut up," he said, and then stomped on the gas. If she mentioned Maggie again he would lock up the brakes and send her flying.

He parked in front of his office instead of behind it to give the rest of the town a good look at Jennifer.

"Okay, lady, here's your new home for a while." He knocked her head against the car as he pulled her out of the back seat.

"You want me to lend your wife a pair of my panties?"

He spun her around and took a swing at her, but even with her hands cuffed behind her back, she was quick and agile enough to sidestep it.

119

"Sheriff," said a guy who'd just come out of the hardware store. "Need a hand there?"

Phillips aimed his finger at the front door and Jennifer walked toward it. "No thanks, Bill. She's a little feisty, but doesn't pose a threat. No reason for her to get hurt."

"Black panties," Jennifer hissed as he pushed her through the entrance. "Nice and silky. You would absolutely *love* them on her."

He shoved her into the cell and slammed the door, then went to his desk and dug at her story that she was a banker back home. Even if someone in England verified it, he didn't believe her, and he hated being in the dark when there was so much at stake. He had to play as smart as her and anticipate any surprise she might throw his way. He couldn't allow her to move the spotlight of guilt away.

What he didn't know about her scared him. Who were her friends back in England and how much political influence might they have? How much clout would it take for her to get the British government involved, perhaps to the point of overseeing the trial and putting pressure on him to be lawful?

He could not allow the cards to be misdealt, and that meant he couldn't let her live long enough to get help from back home. A trial could expose too much. The fabricated pieces he would provide to solve the murders would almost fit, but not quite, and her defense attorney would raise issues that could set her free – leaving unresolved the question of who killed Lenny and Joe.

Phillips didn't have her fingerprints on the knife that killed Joe. He didn't have a sales receipt that tied her to it, and he didn't have a witness or a motive. In fact, other than the facts that she'd bent back Joe's finger and had a bloody knife in her car, there was nothing. A good attorney, hell, even a slacker, could probably get the knife thrown out as fruit of a poisonous tree – inculpating evidence discovered during an illegal search. His grounds for arrest were weak, and no exigent circumstances existed to prevent him from impounding her Expedition and obtaining a court order to search it.

The state's attorney would argue that no foul was committed because the knife would have been discovered upon impound, but he couldn't chance that because if he lost the knife as evidence, a jury would have no choice but to find her not guilty.

That still might be okay, though, because there was a world of difference between being innocent and not being guilty. The town was already sure she'd killed Lenny. She was, after all, the last person seen with him. Jay Stewart had confirmed as much to the guys from the boatyard, and all of them would serve as witnesses. Add their testimony to her breaking Joe's finger and in the town's eyes she would be guilty. At the minimum, she would go back to England and that would end it. He would have solved the case and the murders would stop.

But it was far less risky to set her up properly, arranging the stage so he didn't appear to have a choice, and then kill her. If he did, the worse possible outcome would be an investigation by the state police. But even if they weren't happy with the way he'd handled things, they would overlook the errors because they were cops too. They knew how it was when a criminal broke bad, and understood that sometimes a lethal decision had to be immediate in order to protect the public. He would have prevented the escape of a suspected murderess, so the worst they'd do would be talk to him in private and perhaps suggest a few changes in his prisoner handling procedures.

Phillips would feel a lot better after he'd switched the knife he'd used on Joe with the one from Jennifer's car he was tagging into evidence. But he was the only one with access to either his car's trunk or the evidence locker, so if he didn't want anyone to see them, they wouldn't. It would all be over before anyone examined either knife, but just the same, he wanted the one that skinned Joe tagged as evidence against Jennifer.

He would swap them after the crowd milling around outside went home.

* * *

Jennifer had been taught exactly what to do if she were ever caught as an assassin or spy, but none of that training prepared her for the small town scenario playing out in Buxton. She had confidence in her ability to escape through extraordinary violence, but it seemed a little ridiculous to slit-and-get when all she'd done was bend back a man's finger.

She had a mission to accomplish, though, so if Phillips gave her no choice and pushed hard enough to line up the sights of her conscience, she would kill him in order to get away. She would not disgrace herself simply because she'd managed to get tangled up in a local homicide. Killing her brother, and the seesaw of love and hate on which that mission teetered, was already complicated enough.

It would actually be quite easy for her to kill Phillips. The skirmish of emotions that always took place before making the decision was surprisingly small because he was clearly her enemy, and she definitely had to escape. She could kill him without a big struggle of conscience.

She was, however, still struggling over Phun. Would she kill him or would she falter. Had she inherited a weakness for him from their too-forgiving mother? There was no way to know, and since getting even with Phillips and getting out of jail were far easier objectives, she would be driven by them for now. Phillips had put her life at risk by setting her up and charging her with murder, and she credited him with just enough intelligence to fabricate a compelling case against her. He might even get a conviction in court, sending her to prison or perhaps even the electric chair.

As with all assignments, she'd been briefed on the laws of the countries in which she would be working, the basic information about a criminal's rights or, in those places where bribes were the order of the day, names of those to bribe and the accepted manner in which to do it.

The information in that briefing, all well-intentioned and delivered very confidently by a sharp legal staff who would never dare to test it personally, was sure to prove useless in the uniquely dangerous game she would be playing with Phillips because he controlled not only the game board, but the rules as well, trapping her in a shifty legal position where he had power over all circumstances, or at least he thought he did. It was best for her to help him keep thinking that way, in similar fashion to a game she once played in North Korea and won beautifully. Her Asian ancestry and English beauty would be as useful now as in Korea, where she'd cozied up to a man who knew secrets to which he only referred until she taunted him into backing up his talk with facts she immediately passed via dead drop to her accomplice.

On her last day in-country, soldiers broke down the door of her small room and arrested her with her bags packed, but none of it going anywhere. She spent a week in a shabby prison, and used that time to study the prison's pattern: the movements of the guards, the times for eating, and every other detail that defined the routine. Any disruption in that routine would create a chance to escape, and even a small opportunity could be widened significantly by exploiting the total lack of fear her captors had of such a tiny woman, at least until she unleashed her training and slaughtered everyone between her and the door.

So Jennifer analyzed her new cell the same way, although it was nothing more than a small room behind the sheriff's office with one bar of walls separating it from a narrow hall. She would study the day-to-day rituals and look for anything that might make escape possible. If she understood the patterns, then it would be obvious when something changed, and that change, however slight, would signal her to go, and God help whoever got in her way.

As she counted the sheriff's paces and watched where he moved, she wondered what Phun would do when he learned she was there. Would it matter to him that his sister was charged with the murder he'd so savagely committed? Was he feeling any of the emotional confusion she felt about being near each other after all those years?

He would have to be dead inside not to still feel something for her, and that wasn't possible because he loved his wife and children enough to leave China to avenge them. She knew Phun didn't hate her, even though he must know she'd come to finish him. He could have killed her easily at the boat ramp, but didn't, and that proved he felt something. He had, after all, allowed her and their mother to escape China, and she and Phun would be the only family either of them had after their mother died.

She felt dirty for having spent so many years volunteering for bloody missions in order to qualify for the job of killing a brother who didn't kill her when he had the chance. He had to know she would follow him back to China with deadly intent, but he'd still chosen to let her live.

Had something in her eyes betrayed feelings for him that she hadn't recognized in herself? Did he now believe she wasn't capable of killing him? Had his own emotions interfered, and if so, how far would those emotions extend? Would he go so far as to help her escape, maybe putting an explosive charge against the exterior and blowing the wall? She could easily imagine him doing that, almost as if he were acting in one of those old American westerns they'd watched as kids.

It was far more likely he would poison the food or water or air, or take the sheriff's family and demand an exchange. He had a mind that could come up with many options, but all that mattered to her was whether he would help her or not, and if he did, would she accept it?

That answer was easy. She would accept his help because even if Phillips didn't kill her before her trial, he could probably win a conviction of murder, and that scared her. If she was destined for prison or a gas chamber she wanted it to be for crown and country or love and honor. Bending Joe's finger fell far short, so if Phun decided to help her, yes, she would take it. She would repay the favor by returning to England and telling her boss she could no longer go after him.

By helping her escape, Phun would, in effect, save his own life. At the minimum, he would keep her from being the one to kill him. She would accept her failure because the hate side of the seesaw would be lower than the love side.

It was a relief to think that way, and that confused her even more. Had she really thrown her life away becoming a killer for no other reason than vengeance? That required a guess at the kind of life she'd be living if Phun hadn't killed their father.

She still would have chosen an exciting career and would have never been content being a homemaker, yet even as that ridiculous image passed through her mind it touched her warmly somewhere deep and hopeful and uncomfortable.

If he didn't help her he would still be fair game when she got out of jail, assuming it was in the next few days and not after serving twenty-to-life. She could just see herself as an old-age-pensioner traveling to China with a cane and perhaps a cat carrier, peering over her bifocals to get a better look at the old gits playing chess in the shade at the national grounds in Beijing, looking for her bald and wrinkled brother so she could finally accomplish a mission long forgotten by everyone else.

The sheriff made his usual stop in front of her cell, peered in for about twenty seconds, adjusted his gun belt a half-inch or less, and then walked twelve steps away to the door to his office.

So it was decided. If Phun didn't help her escape she would kill him. With that question put to rest Jennifer wondered how far she was justified in punishing Sheriff Phillips. For reasons she couldn't imagine, he must have killed Joe, or else why was he so anxious to make everyone think she'd done it? That made him a murderer too, and although nothing in her orders sanctioned her killing him, her own sense of justice could easily allow it. Joe had certainly annoyed her in the bar, but he seemed decent enough.

And he must have been Phillips's friend, which made Phillips not only the murderer of an innocent man, but of an innocent *friend*. That was close to killing family, and that made him a target much like her brother. If Phun didn't kill him in order to extricate her, she might have to kill Phillips herself, just to keep the scales in balance for her letting Phun live.

Or perhaps she could trick Phillips into killing Phun for her. If Phillips did that, then of course she would have to forget about retaliating against him for arresting her.

There were lots of moving pieces as she strategized her role in the game that had not yet hit its complexity zenith, and not the least of those pieces was Jay Stewart. The estate agent had set her up, but yet for some stupid reason she also expected him to help her. As unfamiliar as it was for her, she actually liked the idea of him riding into town and saving her from the evil sheriff. It was a silly little schoolgirl fantasy, but she could actually imagine herself sitting back and letting Stewart do all the heavy lifting, then jumping sidesaddle onto his charger and riding off with him.

The phone rang and the sheriff stood to answer it, standing in exactly the same spot he'd stood the last two times, once again leaving open the security door that separated the front office from her single cell in the back, turning away so she couldn't hear his conversation and giving her a three to four second dash to attack him once she manipulated the lock, which was exactly what she was going to do. It had felt nice to mentally unburden herself of the responsibilities she alone would shoulder, but fantasy-time was over. She was ready to go to work as the killer she'd trained so hard to be.

Phillips hung up the phone and walked back through the open door.

"How's the bed, lady. Everything nice and comfy?"

"I'm fine. How's the conscience?"

"Excuse me?"

"How do you feel about slicing up Joe?"

"That's funny, ma'am. I was about to ask you the same thing."

She smiled and got close to the bars. "Come here," she said, barely louder than a whisper.

He stayed back for a minute, then made a small step forward.

"Closer."

He stepped slightly closer.

"Don't be afraid," she said seductively.

"Sorry, ma'am. Close enough. What do you want?"

"Well," she said, and then smiled coyly. "I was just wondering if you've ever seen baby eagles in their nest when there's too little food."

"What?"

"It's just a question, Chief."

"No."

"When food is scarce, the mother can only raise one eagle, so logically you'd think that the other baby would starve, right? But it doesn't. Do you know why?"

"The mother feeds it to the other eagle?"

"Very good, the mother eagle decides which eaglet is stronger and then feeds the weaker eaglet to it. But here's the intriguing part. The surviving baby can't digest real food, so the mother needs to eat it and regurgitate. So there she stands, monstrously un-maternal over the weak little eaglet, little by little shredding pieces off her own baby's tiny skeleton and eating them. The dying eaglet twitches and flaps all the way to its death, but the mother eagle does her work without emotion. The life she's taking is an insignificant cost of survival."

Phillips swallowed. "Your point?"

"I was there when Lenny was butchered in much the same way as the mother eagle butchers her weak baby. I didn't do it, of course, but on the night Lenny died I saw what I just described to you. The emotionless cost of survival in a monster's eyes. Lenny was about your size, wasn't he?"

"About."

"He was as outmatched by his murderer as the eaglet by its mother. Slaughtering Lenny was boring and uneventful for the man who did it, like a dull chore that needed to be done."

"And I suppose you know the man."

"I do."

"And where I can find him?"

"That I don't know."

"Who is he?"

"Chief, I'd be giving you a death sentence if I told you. You'd go after him and die."

"I'm not an idiot, ma'am. I'd take plenty of help."

"Who? You killed Joe and we both know it. I have no idea why, but that leaves you no choice but to be in this alone. Otherwise you run the risk that whoever helps you might discover that Lenny and Joe were killed by two different people, leaving you to explain away Joe's death."

"Even if I went alone, I'd be careful. I'm not new at confrontation."

"Just inexperienced."

"So you say."

"I could be wrong; you might survive. And I might sprout fairy wings and fly out of here. You never know about these things."

She let Phillips worry for most of a minute, and then asked, "Do you plan to kill me today? Or will you wait a few days?"

"Don't know what you're talking about."

"You have to kill me. You've got a crime to cover up before more police or federal authorities get involved."

"You've got one heck of an imagination."

"What happens after I'm dead?"

"I'm afraid that's a question for a priest. Or spiritualist."

"Clever, but the question still stands. What happens to you after I'm dead and someone else gets sliced up? The guy I saw murder Lenny won't hesitate to do it again. He might even start with you, just for fun. Then everyone will know I didn't do it and that you screwed up by killing me – " she cocked her head and fluttered her eyelashes – "a sweet little English girl who hadn't done anything worse than bend back a finger."

Phillips put his hand to his chin as he moved slowly to close the door and shut out his deputy.

"You're a smart lady, I can see that. I can also see there's a lot about you I'll never know. You're too cool behind bars for it to be your first time. I also get the impression you have experience with the legalities that put people behind bars, along with the actions that get them killed before or after they get there. That might make you and me somewhat alike. So tell me, hypothetically, professional cop to professional…whatever, what would you suggest I do so as not to be eaten by the mother eagle?"

"That's simple. Be stronger."

"Than the other eaglet?"

"No. Stronger than the mother eagle."

"It's not possible."

"Chief, we both have something identical in common. Can you tell me what it is?"

"It's Sheriff, God damn it, not Chief. Maybe what's in common is that we're both wasting time talking about this?"

"That's not it, but thanks for the ridiculous answer. What we both risk is being perceived as the weaker eaglet that gets destroyed. Surely even you can see that. I have to worry about you killing me, and you have to worry about Lenny's murderer killing you, but if we combine my knowledge of Lenny's murderer with your presumed ability to kill him, it's possible that together we could become stronger than the mother eagle, capable of eliminating the force that threatens us equally."

The sheriff touched his gun like it was a habit. "And you're sure you know who killed Lenny."

"Of course. And if you kill him, you'll solve Lenny's murder and cover up Joe's at the same time. You *will* have to worry about me, though. How will you know I won't get out of here and tell everyone what you've done?"

"Why don't you tell me?"

"Because, Silly, you have the knife you planted in my car. If I'm not mistaken it's exactly like the one you used to kill Joe, so you can always say Lenny's murderer and I were working together to kill both of them. I can even give you a sworn statement about Lenny's crime scene and how he was ravaged, things no one else could know. You can keep it as insurance."

131

Phillips shook his head as if coming out of a spell. He walked to the door, but before opening it said, "I'll get back with you."

"Fine. I'll be, let's see ..." she checked her wrist where her watch would normally be..."right here when that time comes."

Her laughter made the deputy look up when Phillips opened the door.

9

Stewart had stood way in the back of the Wal-Mart crowd when Phillips took Jennifer away, glad for the instincts that led him to break into Phillips's garage several hours after leaving Joe's house last night. Even with the alarm to bypass and two locks to pick, it was just too easy to steal the knife he'd watch him use on Joe while Phillips was busy boo-hooing to his wife inside.

Compared to all the other secrets, weapons, and people he'd stolen over his career, last night's little break-in and theft meant nothing, yet it still satisfied him on a non-professional, *I-had-a-few-minutes-to-have-fun* level. He'd reset the alarm and relocked everything, so as Phillips stood in front of the crowd waving the knife he'd taken from her car, he certainly felt sure that the other knife was still where he left it, which meant he still thought he owned the game board.

He almost felt sorry for the poor southern sheriff who had no idea of the games Stewart, Jennifer, and Phun were playing around him, but the big sheriff had jumped in willingly and claimed his own lethal foothold, then spiced things up by locking a British agent with an impeccable kill record in his jail. By now she had probably devised a deadly escape plan.

Yet Phillips knew none of that, and that's what made these complicated games of misdirection so much fun. He loved them best when he won in secret without anyone else knowing they'd lost. He'd done it the other way too, but found the feeling far less satisfying.

His worst experience came during his early days with the CIA, immediately before he built the big *Cruiser* reputation he would never manage to live down. He was only twenty-nine, flying over Nicaragua and locating troop movements of the Marxist Sandinistas with his Contra pilot in an old plane that used a car radar detector that was actually fairly efficient, flashing and beeping whenever they were hit by radar.

About an hour into the flight it lit up solid and buzzed steady. Someone had them locked on, so the pilot, who was late teens but already seasoned by conflict, rolled the plane and dove for the ground. The buzzing stopped just before they ran out of altitude, and as they leveled off above the treetops and headed for base a barrage of small arms fire ripped through the cockpit and killed the pilot.

The engine caught fire and fuel sprayed from the wing tanks as Cruiser fought the auxiliary controls and looked for an empty patch of ground. He was too low to glide far and couldn't stretch it out or he would stall and crash. There wasn't any place to land but jungle. He felt stupid wondering which tree would be the softest to hit but thought it anyway, then picked a big canopy ahead on the right, pushed the rudder over, aimed just above it, and then pulled back on the yoke so that the plane climbed briefly before crashing into the top of the tree with enough force to throw Cruiser forward, his face hitting the yoke and cracking with dozens of snapping sounds that were the last noises he heard.

His next memory was of being in a bed, but not at a hospital. He was in a small tent with a young guard standing over him.

"He's awake," the guard shouted in Spanish.

Several men rushed in while Cruiser tried to focus through his left eye. His right didn't work. He lifted a hand to his face and touched bandages. He dabbed around and felt them everywhere. His left eye was the only spot exposed.

"Where ..." he tried to ask, but broken bones moved around in his face and he passed out.

It was dark when he woke again. He could hear a vehicle, heavy and large, diesel, and five...no six, voices. A communications radio crackled nearby, so he must be near the command tent. He passed out again before he could interpret.

The next time he woke, an older man, bald, sixty, civilian clothes, was snipping the wrapping off his face.

"Be still, my friend. I don't want to cut you." The man looked both horrified and pleased as the bandages came off. Cruiser knew he was hurt bad, but the drugs controlled the pain so he tried to talk. Without the bandages, his jaw fell open with the sound of breaking twigs. The doctor's face showed that he felt the pain too.

They moved him several times over the next two months. Everything seemed to be healing, but nothing in his face seemed to be in the same spot as before the crash. Sandinista officers would come in every day and give him a pen and pad and ask him questions, demanding answers in exchange for his life and the care they provided.

Cruiser was too weak to write, and pretended to be long after he wasn't. When they threatened violence, the old doctor threw them out. The doc had ultimate power because they would need him when they were the one to get shot.

One day the doctor leaned over Cruiser and whispered, "Soon you must tell them something. You're strong enough to write and they know it. Tell them anything, my friend, even a good lie."

That night he heard on their radio that the Contras were getting close, which explained why most men had left the camp to establish another base. They were coming back tomorrow for the wounded, the prisoners, and the men who guarded them, so this was going to be his best chance, even if he wasn't ready to take it. They didn't expect such an injured man to fight, so they only had one guard outside each end of the tent. If he waited until he was stronger, he would be at the new camp with more soldiers, and his improved health would justify additional guards.

Cruiser had only one experience with killing back then, and that was all a reaction to someone trying to kill him first. This would be different. He could only guess how outnumbered he was, but even a dozen people meant he had to assume everyone was a threat. With little peripheral vision to his left and none to his right, he would have to fire immediately at anything that caught his attention.

The camp was always quiet at night, so he waited until he heard the snoring that came a few hours after darkness. He could smell a guard smoking behind his tent, but the soldier in front was asleep.

Pain shot through Cruiser's chest as he rolled onto his stomach, and without thinking he bit his lip to keep from screaming. That shifted the healing bones in his face, which hurt horribly, but he locked down his scream and focused on transforming pain into fury as his knees touched the ground. He rested a few seconds, unbelievably tired but getting stronger as the anticipation of a now-or-never moment pumped the first drops of adrenaline into his system.

He looked deeper inside himself than ever before, searching for the savagery that would enable him to administer pain and death. He corralled it and gave it absolute rein, blocking out fear and sympathy and compassion and anything else that might be good. He dipped himself into the black pit of pure evil, leaving no place for even the smallest amount of goodness because it could be as much an enemy as the Sandinistas he had to kill.

He stood up awkwardly and almost fainted, but he wouldn't allow his body to do it. He took five steps, each one a little smoother than the last as he moved toward the end of his tent where the guard slept. He lifted back the tent flap. The camp was quiet and dark.

He reached for the rifle he hoped would be fully loaded, and just as he got his hand on the weapon the soldier woke, looked up casually and saw Cruiser. Then he screamed.

Cruiser spun the rifle around and shot him in the head at zero range, then aimed through his tent and shot the hot glow of the cigarette at the other end. He hobbled toward the jungle as panic swept the camp like a wave and naked soldiers stumbled out of tents. They saw Cruiser and fired dozens of rounds that hit all around until he dropped clumsily behind a log and fired back at everything that moved. He killed men who shot at him and he killed men who didn't. He saw men running away and he killed them too. They were all enemies. They had to be. There was no time to sort them out.

Cruiser killed the man who dashed out of the tent nearest his, realizing too late that he was another prisoner trying to escape. He watched him wobble and fall, just for a second of the high-octane moment as the doctor came out of his tent and hollered for all of them to stop shooting, yelling at Cruiser, promising that no one would shoot at him as he ran.

Cruiser would always remember the doctor's exact words. They seemed to have traveled slowly to him that night, not nearly fast enough for him to process in time to keep from shooting.

He killed the doctor just as his words made sense. *Run into the jungle. I'm trying to help you.*

Everyone else must have understood, though, because they stopped firing long enough for Cruiser to escape into the darkness. He limped as far away as he could and hid until the Contras came late the next day. They counted eleven dead bodies, and celebrated Cruiser's ruthlessness as they took him back to their camp, heralding the white-bandaged warrior in ways that seemed destined for history. From there he went to Puerto Rico for reconstructive surgery on his face.

He would never forgive himself for repaying the doctor's care and compassion with a bullet. As far as he knew, none of the men he'd slaughtered that night had ever hurt him, and he would never even know if they wanted to be there, if they were zealots or conscripts. But they were there and so he'd killed them, simple as that.

Langley wanted to count all the bodies as covert kills since it wasn't a declared war, just some warring factions battling for supremacy. The United States wasn't supposed to have men in combat there, so that meant those kills qualified as covert.

Cruiser insisted that each and every one of the men he'd killed were military targets, and threatened all kinds of things to make the classification stick.

"Five," he'd said firmly, *again*, when it came up last month. "Five specific covert targets. Can't count collateral damage or military firefights, and definitely can't count assassinated political leaders."

"They all count," Nick countered, as always. "Hell, go ahead and leave out the declared conflicts and you're still only one kill away from beating the Agency record – and that record includes the bloody days of Vietnam."

"Like I didn't end up bloody in –"

"I haven't heard you refer to Nicaragua in years."

"I want to retire on the uphill side of that record, so keep it at five."

"It's not the truth."

"The truth would chain me to a lethal reputation and you know it. Just like Adams. Let him be Mr. Big."

Whether they admitted it or not, everyone knew that anything other than a specific target was a mistake. Innocents only died when someone was careless. Shooting it out with an enemy meant a mission had been exposed. Assassinations were the biggest mistakes of all because they meant the Agency had failed to orchestrate an overthrow of whatever leader stood in America's way. So bragging about those deaths was nothing more than a way to disguise the failings.

One of his innocent victims – accidental or unintended deaths being the only *innocent victims* and therefore the ones who haunted him – was a homeless man in a Bratislavian alley that Cruiser killed with two silenced shots that burned through the worn coat and into his dirty body. Twelve years later Cruiser still beat himself up over his bad preparation that lead to the death, and ever since then he'd taken all the time necessary to plan his attacks flawlessly, reaching a level of complexity that absolutely frustrated his boss in Virginia.

The wind was getting serious as he sat on a bench in front of Buxton's True Value hardware store, next to the Dip-n-Sip donut shop and across the street from the sheriff's office. He stood up when a hearse turned the corner and idled down the street, followed by a single limousine carrying Lenny's ex-wife.

"Oh, my," said a woman on the sidewalk behind him. "That was fast."

Everyone on the street stopped what they were doing. People came out of the hardware store and set down the lumber and supplies they'd bought in preparation for the hurricane. The barber came out of his shop and the guy he was shaving followed, the cape still hanging around his neck. In the grand tradition of small towns, they stood at attention as the hearse eased by, showing their respect for the end of a life.

"He was cremated," a fisherman said under his breath. "Linda was in The Harpooner last night celebrating because Lenny left everything to her. The insurance business, everything. Asked her to take care of the funeral too, and I guess cremation was cheapest and quickest."

"I didn't even hear about it. The poor man won't have hardly anyone at the grave."

"Said she wanted him resting in peace before the hurricane hit 'cause it's going to be a whopper. She didn't want to worry about how long his body would keep if the power stayed off."

The fisherman put his hand over his heart as the hearse passed. As Lenny's ex-wife's limousine followed, the old man lowered his hand and spit, then stepped into the street and walked behind it.

The barber joined him, along with the customer who wiped the shaving cream onto the cape and folded it as best he could while the strengthening wind snapped at it. By the end of the block a dozen citizens of the town that had always rejected Lenny were escorting him to his final resting place, and on a very personal level that gave Stewart a great deal of hope for his own future in Buxton.

When the procession rounded a corner three blocks away, Stewart went back to work on that future, separating the details of the game and prioritizing the outcomes. First and foremost, Phun was still in town, but since he now knew that he hadn't killed the murderer of his family, Stewart could afford to let him dangle at least as long as Jennifer was safely locked away in jail. He didn't know if she was ready to kill her brother, but he couldn't chance that happening until he could tie Sheriff Phillips to Phun in order to neatly wrap up all the deaths.

His biggest worries were that Phun might go after Phillips for framing Jennifer, or that Jennifer might kill Phillips in order to escape. Either would destroy months if not years of work.

He had to keep Phillips alive until Phun was dead so that a connecting thread ran through all the deaths, creating a logical connection that eliminated a terrorist threat to the United States, ended the string of local murders, satisfied the locals, and put his adopted town at peace. If Phillips died out of sequence, the murders of Lenny and Joe would appear to remain unsolved.

He could already hear Nick bitching that "once again you've made the game way too complicated" but he always made the same complaint so it not only didn't matter anymore, it had more or less become a game to keep Nick in the dark.

Jennifer was the only person he didn't worry about because she could take care of herself. If she decided that escape was the only way to avoid a prison term or death, the sheriff and his deputy would be no match for the excellent work of which she was capable. She might even eclipse his reputation if she stayed in the trade and lived long enough.

He wondered if she had any idea what that life would cost her, and spent a few seconds placing value on what it would cost him if she stayed in the game after Buxton. Was there anything to the feelings she stirred in him, and if so, how long would he wait for her to figure out that the road she traveled was a dead end?

It shocked him how easily he considered the idea of waiting for her. On the rare occasions when that kind of thing happened it usually signaled something genuine, and what could be more genuine than the desire to share his life with someone. So should Stewart create some doubt in her mind about being a spy, maybe tell her that loneliness would always be her worst enemy?

With the beautiful exception of his brief time with Simone, Stewart had always worked alone, with no one sharing his career or his life and no one really giving a shit about him. He had long ago learned to accept that, but it hadn't been easy.

But over the last few years it had fostered a sadness that kept forcing its way to the front of his mind as he watched happy couples together. It was almost a hobby, perhaps an obsession, something he wanted badly for himself but might never have. He wondered if Jennifer was strong and foolish enough to make that kind of long-term sacrifice for nothing more than a job. If so, she probably had a great professional future ahead of her, and she wouldn't be sidetracked by a simple country sheriff she could kill without breaking a nail.

"Hello," said an older man who sat down on the bench with him, holding his cap against the wind. "Ready for the hurricane?"

"Suppose so. How well does the sheriff enforce the governor's evacuation order?"

Stewart wanted as many people as possible safely out of the way when he fought Phun. Of course, Sheriff Phillips wouldn't leave, and neither would Jennifer. The road would be closed and all the island's killers would be isolated. If everyone else left, Stewart could work without attracting any attention at all.

"He pushes you to leave, but doesn't pull you out. I'm not going anywhere. Still need batteries, but my wife's inside getting 'em now." He looked at the sky and smiled. "I love watching this bad weather coming. Down at the beach you can see a great mass of darkness spinning out over the ocean."

"How was the surf?"

"Big. Seems to be getting bigger by the moment."

Even with all he had going on, Stewart thought about the hurricane's deep ocean swells eventually cresting into the shallow water surrounding the island. Perhaps that was because it was the future, and placing him in the future always did a good job of tricking him into believing he'd be there to see it.

"Hurricane's gonna howl and rip at this island, but I've been through bunches of 'em. At some point even the meanest of 'em loses energy."

143

"And once the eye passes," Stewart said, more to himself than the old man, "the wind will shift to offshore and do something unbelievable."

"You love this too, don't you?"

"Mostly those last few hours, when that wind holds up the very waves it created. Especially if they're huge and clean. Maybe even rideable."

"Rideable? You mean to surf? Think I'll give that one a pass."

They both laughed, and then the man's wife came out and looked at Stewart. The old boy made a try at introductions but his wife pulled him up by the arm and hurried them away, saying "That man was with the woman who killed Joe" without even trying to keep Stewart from hearing.

According to the National Weather Service, the hurricane had picked up speed and would roar ashore in about twelve hours. It would be gone by tomorrow, so it was time for work.

The deputy walked out of the sheriff's office, probably going to lunch. Stewart stood as the young police officer walked across the street toward him. He needed a quick read on him, and this was his first real chance to get it.

"How are you today, Deputy?"

The deputy made a point of not looking up or saying anything to the man so negatively associated with Jennifer. He just kept walking until he rounded the corner and got blasted by the wind. Then Stewart walked over to the sheriff's office. The door was locked, but after he jiggled the handle, Phillips opened it.

You," he said. "What do you want?"

"Let's talk."

"About what?"

Stewart didn't answer because although Phillips was a lawman, he was also a criminal who'd murdered in cold blood. Stewart expected the curious guilt of his criminal side to rule, forcing Phillips to let him in.

The sheriff stepped outside and looked up and down the sidewalk. There wasn't anyone nearby but there could have been, so he was acting the way Stewart expected. For all Phillips knew Stewart could be part of a setup, working with someone in a car across the street who might be listening with headphones and a powerful directional microphone. Or Stewart might be wearing a wire.

The sheriff looked Stewart over. Then he stepped aside and let him walk past.

"I've done some checking on you, Mr. Stewart. You're not exactly what you pretend to be." Phillips took a last look outside before closing the door.

"Is that right? Why would you bother?"

"There's something about you I don't like. It pays to know my enemies."

Stewart moved around the office, examining things just to make Phillips uncomfortable. As he read a commendation on the wall he asked, "What was it about me that mystified you, Sheriff?"

"Never said I was mystified, but you're not the sissy you pretend to be as that woman leads you around town. You've got an impressive record in the military police. I'm surprised you didn't go into law enforcement after you retired from the Army instead of being a Realtor."

"You checked me out because you think I'm a sissy? Odd. Were you threatened by that?"

"I don't get threatened. I get suspicious. Anytime someone new comes to town, I check 'em out. Especially if they remind me of someone I don't like."

"Who might that be?"

"Doesn't matter. Slight resemblance, but he wasn't born in Nebraska."

"Cornhusker state."

"Who cares? What do you want?"

"Well, Trent…you mind if I call you Trent?"

"Sheriff works just fine."

"You've got an innocent woman back there. I know it, she knows it, and I'm pretty sure you know it too."

"Found what I believe to be the murder weapon in her car. Had blood on it. How can you be so sure?"

"Because she was with me. I was waiting in her room when you followed her home last night. Later on we laughed about making love while the law was outside in the dark doing…well, whatever it was you did out there in the dark."

"That's a lie and not even a good one. She murdered Joe. I'll be able to prove that."

"I can get the motel's phone records and prove we were there when Joe was murdered. Assuming it was before I left around four."

"Maybe you can prove *you* were there. Doesn't mean she was."

"She called her mother in England. And left a message at work."

"I'll check it out."

"The sooner the better. The less egg you'll have on your face."

"Eggs only come with my breakfast."

"We'll see."

"A sissy," Stewart said, and then smiled. "I think I like that."

He walked to the door leading to the cell. "Can I talk to her for a minute? It won't change the phone records or anything. I just don't want her to think I'm not trying to help."

Phillips's hand was at his chin, as it had been since Stewart mentioned the phone calls. "Don't see it as doing any harm. If she's innocent, I'm certainly willing to admit a mistake."

"Thank you."

Stewart thought the sheriff would come over and search him like he would anyone visiting a murder suspect, but he just waved Stewart in. And why shouldn't he? He knew Jennifer wasn't a murderess, so he would naturally feel he had nothing to fear. Innocent people didn't normally attempt jailbreaks.

The door to the cell area was unlocked so Stewart opened it and walked through. Jennifer was sitting on her bunk. She looked through the bars without emotion.

"Hi, I'm –"

"Keep your voice down," she said. "There's a microphone in here somewhere."

"I know," he said quietly, "I heard you humming. Look, I told the sheriff we were in your motel room making love when Joe was murdered. I also told him about the phone calls that will prove you were there."

She raised an eyebrow and seemed intrigued. "You told him we made love?"

"It was terrific."

"I'm sure I was. How were you?"

He was embarrassed, and amazed she could be so relaxed while in jail. But if she could make fun out of this, then he could take a second to enjoy it too.

147

"To be honest, I carried the slack for you, but you were okay. It was good enough for a first time and all."

"I was just okay? Jay, if you ever make love to me and I'm just okay, you'd better turn on the light and see who you're really with."

Stewart wanted to laugh because she really was a cool player. They'd moved closer as they talked, and so right then, when they were both smiling and enjoying the moment, he whispered very softly, "I've got the knife that killed Joe. The *real* one, not the duplicate I planted in your car."

Everything about her changed: her posture, the look on her face, and the confidence in her eyes. He'd confused her several times since they'd met, but now the look was absolute.

"What did you just say? Why did you plant that knife in my car?"

"Shh. I needed you to provide a distraction for me. Don't worry, though, because I won't let you go to jail over it."

She held up her hands to remind him of her surroundings, gritted her teeth and strained to stay quiet. "I'm *already* in jail over it."

"This isn't jail. You know what I mean, prison. I've got you covered."

"Oh now I feel better."

Sheriff Phillips came in like he'd been hovering just outside the door. "What are you two talking about? This whispering makes me think you lied to me out there, Mr. Stewart."

Stewart looked at Jennifer. "Trust me, okay? I've got to go."

He'd done what he had to do, so as he turned to leave he thanked Sheriff Phillips for his time.

* * *

Jennifer tried not to show her confusion over Stewart's mentioning the knife, but Phillips surely must have seen it. As he escorted Stewart out he kept looking back as though he couldn't wait to see what had her upset.

So she tried to reset herself and think professionally, but Stewart had dealt her three in a row and that made it hard. She had no idea what role Cruiser had played in Stewart's actions, but she knew he had a part in them.

She had to consider that Stewart might have killed Joe. Otherwise how could he have the knife? He'd already acted like he might be involved in something illegal, but she didn't want him to be a killer cold-blooded enough to slice up someone as small and harmless as Joe.

Stewart had impressed her with his cunning, so he was definitely complex enough to be a good criminal, perhaps even a traitor who sold his Army knowledge to whoever wrote the biggest check. So perhaps Cruiser had come to Buxton to ferret him out.

Friend or enemy, it made good sense to try to understand him. Had he set her up that morning in the restaurant? Yes, definitely. Did he have the knife that killed Joe? Apparently. Did he have motive or opportunity? Who knew?

But if he *had* killed Joe, why had he told her about the knife, almost admitting the murder to her? For that matter, why had he planted a duplicate knife in her Expedition and then confessed to doing it?

Had he been an officer or enlisted in the Army? Had he ever been in battle, and if so, how had he done? Had he married? What happened to his wife? Did he have kids?

149

How did he get the scars that still traced subtly across his face? Had he grown his beard to cover even worse scars on his cheeks and jaw? Did he exercise to stay in such good shape or was he merely genetically lucky?

She rubbed her shoulders like it was cold in the cell. Maybe it was seeing her brother, or being locked up again, but for some reason she was way too aware of being alone. She was a killer, but also a woman with the same hopes as other women. She just kept them locked away, and sometimes the lock broke.

Sheriff Phillips came back with the knife Stewart said he had put in her car as a distraction. It was the first time she'd seen it up close and she was surprised to see so much blood on it.

"Okay, little eaglet," Phillips said, "I've been thinking about what you said and agree it's time we teamed up."

He turned the lock but didn't open her door. He stepped back and waited for her to walk out, but she wouldn't. She wasn't sure if he was playing the kill-her-in-an-escape-attempt game or not, so she held the door in place and said, "I suppose you want to know who killed Lenny."

"I think that's what we talked about."

Jennifer thought it all through while Phillips waited. Could she count on her brother to help her? Of course not. And despite her growing feelings toward Stewart, he had set her up *again* by planting the knife, so she sure wouldn't count on him.

That left it completely her responsibility to get herself out of jail and back to her mission to kill Phun, even though she was fast losing interest in doing it, which made her ask if she'd gone so soft so quickly because of a few silly emotions? Was she really considering walking away from her career, and if so, was she quitting because she was down on points or because she wanted a lot more out of her life?

She definitely wasn't a quitter, yet she was certainly confused. For a brief time she'd felt more complete than she had during even the best days with Nigel. She'd seen her brother and discovered she still cared about him. She'd met a new man for whom she actually felt something, which meant she'd had two important men in her life for a wonderful instant. But now Stewart had double-crossed her, proving once again that she should never trust her instincts about men.

So as Phillips waited, she realized how much she did not want to kill Phun, because if he died she would be alone. She'd sworn for years to kill him, but as she stood in her cell she realized that she liked the idea of sitting down and talking with him, catching up on the last few decades, expressing regret that his family – which was her family, too – had died so violently.

She could only comprehend those feelings because of the fact that Phun hadn't hurt her or set her up, which stood in sharp contrast to what Stewart had done. She was in jail because he'd put her there, and that put him directly across the battlefield whether she wanted him there or not. Yes, she liked him, and yes, he said he was trying to help, but if he hadn't set her up in the first place she wouldn't need the help.

Maybe she'd been wrong about Phillips being an idiot and corrupt. Maybe he was just like her, doing his job the best way he knew, making an occasional mistake but overall getting it mostly right.

"I want to know who killed Lenny," Phillips finally asked, a little forcefully because of the wait. "Or perhaps you never did know."

Wes DeMott

Jennifer couldn't slow the situation down enough for her feelings to align with Stewart's betrayal. Perhaps he was another Nigel and she would never understand why he would hurt her, and certainly not before she missed her best chance at escape. It made her sad to give up on whatever might have been between them, but it was the intelligent thing to do, especially with the sheriff losing patience.

"Forget it," he said. "I'll go check your phone records. If they don't clear you, you're toast." He clicked his teeth together and made a sound like a steak hitting a hot grill. "We've got the death penalty in this state."

"The man who killed Lenny just left, Sheriff."

She'd blurted it out, something she seldom did without *wanting* to sound like she'd blurted out important information, but hell, why should she be ashamed of that? She no longer felt anything like a professional, but like a pawn in everyone else's game: Stewart's, the sheriff's, perhaps even her brother's. And since pawns had little power to cause much damage, she wouldn't worry about who would paid the consequences.

"You're kidding. That guy?"

"He has the knife that killed Joe. The one you found in my car was a decoy."

Phillips looked stunned and she suddenly felt terrible because all the evidence didn't cancel out her instinct to trust Stewart. Sure, she wanted to even the score with him, but if her instincts were right, this was clearly overkill.

"You don't say. This knife's a decoy. And he's got the real one?"

"He says he does."

"Did he happen to say how he got it?"

"I guess he had it before he used it on Joe. Or do you mean you already know that someone else killed Joe and

152

you're just wondering how Stewart got the knife from them?"

Phillips looked suddenly on trial and unwilling to help the prosecutor by answering, so he wandered out to his office and sat down at his desk. He was muttering when he seemed to realize that she was still in her cell.

"Well go on. Get out of here. Just don't leave Buxton."

"Ever?"

"Just don't do it yet. We're not done, you and me."

"Will you tell Stewart what I told you?"

"That's not your concern."

"We're in this nest together, Sheriff, trying to be stronger than the eagle hovering over us. Work with me."

"Work with you? Fine. Come here."

He opened the evidence bag and held it out. "Reach in and put your fingerprints all over the knife. You're right-handed?"

"Yes."

"Then use your right hand. If you double-cross me...s-s-s-s-s-s, it's the electric chair for you."

She hesitated. If she did, she could go out the door and all the way back to England where a host of foreign secretaries could protect her. She no longer cared about finding Cruiser or doing her mission. She'd made a mess of it and wanted to go home, forget about Phun, forget about Stewart, and forget about Buxton. Get another assignment and get on with her career, or quit and get on with her life. But first she had to get through the sheriff's door, and handling the knife was her ticket. So she did.

Phillips sealed the bag. "That guy's not a powerful eagle, not by a long shot. He's a sissy I can handle alone. You'll see. He'll be...well, let's just say I'll have him handled before morning."

"Maybe, Sheriff," she said as she walked slowly to the door and turned the knob. The wind slammed it into her and it hurt, but the fresh air tasted good after the staleness of her cell. "Maybe," she repeated, not even trying to conceal her uncertainty about so many things.

She stepped outside and had trouble pulling the door closed. She leaned into the wind as she started down the sidewalk. When she got near the corner, Stewart pulled up in his Jeep.

"Want a ride?"

She looked back at the sheriff's office. Phillips was watching her through the window.

"No thanks. I'll walk."

He idled along beside her. "You told the sheriff what I said, didn't you?"

She kept walking but turned to see his face. He looked hurt and it hurt her right back. "Why would I do that?"

"To get out. You *are* out, so that's pretty strong evidence. At least admit what you've done so I'll know what I'm dealing with."

He pulled to the curb and stopped.

She looked around at the front yards of slash pines and magnolias, the azaleas and dogwoods lining the sidewalk and bending to the wind, contrasting the beauty of the little town to all the ugly mistakes she'd made there.

"Why shouldn't I have told him? You crazy idiot, you planted evidence that got me arrested. You say you have the murder weapon, which means you were probably the one to use it. Why should I worry about protecting you?"

He dropped his head. "I don't know. I thought you knew I liked you. I hoped you would trust that I really was trying to help."

She leaned into the open window. "By planting a knife in my car?"

"By getting you out. I lied. I didn't plant the knife in your car. I'm sure Phillips did. From what I could see from a distance it looks just like the one he used on Joe."

She opened the door slowly and climbed in without taking her eyes off Stewart.

"You know for a fact that Phillips killed Joe?"

He slid one of the photos he'd taken last night across the seat. "Don't tell me you didn't suspect him already?"

"He's a terrible man."

"So you told him what I said?"

She didn't take her eyes off him, but she didn't speak either.

"Well, it seems to have worked. You got out. That's what I wanted."

She threw her head back against the seat and stared at the ceiling. "God, I was so *stupid* in there. Now he thinks you killed Joe…no," she turned and looked for help. "I guess he doesn't, does he? He knows that he killed Joe, so …"

"See? I'm not in any danger."

"How did you know to be there? How did you get the knife?"

"You think I just broke up bar fights in the Army? I learned a trick or two."

"Oh. Then what do you know about Lenny's murder?"

"Can't help you there. Does the sheriff still think you killed him?"

"I'm not sure."

"It's ridiculous if he does. You'd just met him. What would be your motive? Besides, if he really suspected you, he wouldn't have let you go."

155

"Jay, I screwed up. I touched the knife, the one he took out of my car."

He hit the brakes especially hard and slid to a stop. "You did what? What in the world were you thinking?"

"Phillips made me. It was stupid, I know. I just wanted out of there. I want to go home and forget all about this."

Stewart didn't say anything as he slid his foot off the brake and drove away. She didn't say anything either, although she wanted to apologize for acting with the haste and confusion of an amateur, because by doing so she'd put Stewart's life at risk. Phillips's eyes had said what his statement implied, that before morning he would kill the only man she'd been attracted to in years.

She reached over and touched his hand. "I'm sorry."

Stewart looked at her hand but didn't touch her back. "No big deal. If he does come around and arrest me, I can prove I'm innocent and he'll look incompetent. Then the state police will take over and figure out he killed Joe. Maybe Lenny. Who knows?"

She wanted to tell him that Phillips was planning to kill him but it was just too much to admit. So she stared out her window and said "You're probably right. God, I really hope you're right."

10

Sand blasted Phun's face as he forced his way along the ravaged beach, impressed as always with the incredible power of nature – the only force he could ever admire without feeling challenged. Howling winds pushed the dark grey sky in a slow-moving swirl while massive waves lined up as far out in the ocean as he could see and marched like flanks of giant soldiers toward war. They were bigger than even an hour ago, and when the waves hit shore they surged up the beach and chewed away at the dunes, creating wide run-outs as the water channeled back to the Atlantic.

He was surprised to see other people struggling along the beach, but not because there was an evacuation order. It was already clear that the islanders stoically rode out the storms of their lives, so whether through bravery or stupidity, Phun couldn't imagine them abandoning their homes and making a run for safety. He grudgingly respected their willingness to strap themselves down on a narrow spit of land jutting far into the Atlantic.

Their strength made him question his hatred of Americans as lazy and self-indulgent, and forced him to remember that his battle was with the American government and not the people. But the easiest way to damage the government was to destroy millions of its people, even some decent ones. Blood had always been the currency of freedom, and the U.S. needed to spill barrels of it if China was to stay free of its influence.

A small group of young men came over the dunes and stared at the surf. One of them shouted to Phun over the noise of the wind. "You surf, dude?"

Phun decided to depart from a lifetime of tradition and shouted back "No" to the ordinary person.

"You see how the wind is blowing the waves over and closing them out?"

"You mean breaking them without pure form."

The surfer laughed. "Sure. Wacky way of saying it, but yeah. By daybreak the eye of the hurricane will have passed, and when that happens the wind will shift around to the other direction."

"And?"

"And? Man, it's going to hold these waves up until they're giants. They'll try to break but the wind will make them keep standing, and the longer that happens the bigger they'll get."

"I see."

"Then you should come back in the morning and see something awesome, especially if anyone has the guts to paddle out and surf. Judging from their size now, it's going to be seriously out of control."

Phun was glad the young man had spoken to him, friendly enough but not really caring whether Phun spoke back or not. That made it easy because they were just two strangers watching nature make the ocean do things that man, with all his skill and resources, could never dream of doing.

He felt small as the wind pushed him around and ripped at his clothes. Not small in stature but small in importance, minor in the presence of the god in which he didn't believe, insignificant in a way he'd seldom felt as he ruled his life from his fortress-like compound, surrounded by loyal soldiers and a devoted staff.

What did he have to show for the years he'd traded for a political ideal that his short time in America made him think might, in fact, have flaws? What made him so sure of himself when a mere wind, invisible and indiscriminate, could push him around like a kite, making him weave and flutter like the ordinary people on the beach with him?

Those doubts, his dead family, and the solitude of the beach made him sad for the isolation of his life, and marvel that Jennifer was so close at the very time he felt so alone. Was it an interesting coincidence that they'd crossed separate oceans at the same time to end up in the same little town?

No, he knew why she was there, but he preferred to think a good spirit had sent her to help him, just like she always tried to help by understanding both his and their father's sides of an argument. She always respected Phun for believing so strongly in his cause, but as soon as she found out he'd killed someone, she turned her back on him.

Now she too was a killer, shedding blood for her beliefs just like him. He knew everything she'd done with the Royal Marines and knew the rumors about her work in MI5 and 6, although the details were just as much a mystery as how she knew to find him in Buxton.

She hadn't made a move against him when he killed Lenny, but there was no doubt that she'd come to kill him. That made *her* the vicious one who wanted to shed blood for her beliefs, while he was there nobly seeking the kind of

159

justice everyone on the planet could understand – honoring his family by slaying their killer.

But killing the black man hadn't felt noble, even before he found out he was an innocent man. Phun normally would have gloried in the battle and howled in his victory, but that night his sister's presence added emotions he'd never felt before. He'd hoped to impress her but she was horrified. He'd thrown her on the ground and she sat there watching with her own cold eye of a killer, yet showed no appreciation for the skill and power he displayed for her.

He should have waited until she'd dropped the man off at his Mercedes because other than a mother he would never see again, Jennifer was the last of his family. Now he'd pushed her almost as far out of reach as the dead wife and children he wished he'd known better. He'd blatantly defied his government to have a second child, and would now give his entire fortune to sit with his daughter and discuss the dancing she loved, or take his son fishing or hiking, something other than the martial arts Phun insisted they did in spite of the boy's reluctance.

And he would trade life itself for the chance to do something personal for his wife, maybe send the staff away and cook a nice meal for her. She would have loved that, and would probably have cried until whatever he made got cold. He smiled as he thought about that, but the smile disappeared as he remembered her obliterated body. He would never have the chance to cook her anything. She would never again cry or smile.

Through that sadness he saw the truth that what killed his family was the way he lived. In a sad and terribly harsh way, *he* was *Sha Hai Wo Jia de Shung Shou*. Two nights ago he was sure the black man was Cruiser, the man who destroyed his family and his life, yet killing a thousand

Cruisers wouldn't have killed the man who caused the deaths of family.

It was strange thinking for him, the kind of cerebral exercise over which he used to ridicule his father. Perhaps maturity was finally descending on him, supporting his father's theory that a wise man measures his life in transformations rather than years.

The wind gusted and pushed him down onto the beach where the sand tore fiercely at his face. The wind had been clever to exploit his inattention as he thought of his dead family, and that proved that it was a weakness without purpose and not to be tolerated. They were dead. He couldn't change that by suffering for them in this strange land where he felt less a stranger each day.

He forced his way onto his feet and then stood there shouting at the wind, daring it to knock him down again and just as determined not to let it.

* * *

Sheriff Phillips couldn't wait to find out if the knife he used on Joe was really missing from his trunk. The sidewalk outside his office was busy with people rushing back from Lenny's funeral, but they were all in a hurry to finish their preparations for the storm, and except for the young hardware clerk coming his way with a piece of plywood, paid little attention to him

"Hey, Sheriff, looks like she's going to make landfall at Duck." The kid fought the wind as he slid the plywood into a pickup next to Phillip's patrol car. "They ain't for sure, though. A little wobble and who knows where it'll hit."

"You staying, Bobby?"

"Yes, sir. Having me a hurricane party at my dad's house."

"If it heads right at us, don't be too drunk to help out with cleanup afterward. You and your folks should probably leave now."

He knew Bobby wouldn't leave. The people who'd moved onto the island since the last big hurricane would most likely be scared enough to leave, but long time folks had to be pried loose.

"You leaving, Sheriff?"

"You know I can't."

"Then me neither. I'll go when you do. Same with my dad."

"Better inflate your water wings, then. Seen the waves?"

"Done it already, and made five hundred bucks last night helping folks haul boats or make 'em secure. Well, better get back inside. Almost out of plywood and batteries so might get off early. Be cool, Sheriff."

As Bobby left, Phillips popped the trunk, holding the lid so the wind didn't blow it off. He grabbed the bag where he'd hidden the knife, but it was gone, no question about it. He could see a note inside the bag so he carried it back to his office, locked the door, and then pulled out the note with tweezers.

"You can get your knife back tonight in the driveway of Captain Dave's condemned house. Midnight, not one minute earlier."

It had to be from Stewart. He'd told Jennifer he had the knife, so he must have been the one to steal it. Phillips tried to think like a cop instead of a killer and consider if it could have been taken by his deputy, his own son, or maybe even Lenny's real murderer – God, how easy it was to forget there was another killer on the island. But all arrows pointed to Stewart.

If Stewart had his knife he probably knew he'd killed Joe with it. He could have even been out at Joe's house, and to make matters worse, he'd probably told that to Jennifer when Phillips foolishly allowed him to visit her in jail.

Maybe he'd even told the state police. He put himself in Stewart's shoes and that's exactly what he would have done.

Stewart hadn't done that, though, because the state police hadn't shown up. Instead, he'd asked for a meeting to give the knife back. That meant a trade. What did Stewart want badly enough to let Phillips get away with murder?

Had Stewart been the one to kill Lenny, and now wanted to make a deal that left that murder unsolved? Had Jennifer done it, and did Stewart want the same thing for her? Maybe neither of them had done a damned thing and just wanted to change their status back to non-suspects so they could go on with their lives, even if it meant letting Phillips get away with murder.

He wished Jennifer was still locked up. It would have been reasonable for him to hold her as a suspect and he could certainly have stretched it out a few more days. If he had, he could now use her as leverage against Stewart.

"Baby eaglets, my ass," he muttered. "She was in this with him, no doubt. Maybe even the one in charge."

He hated being played, but in small town law enforcement the rules of the game could change at any time. He'd learned that from his dad, who always said that's where the fun of being sheriff came in, using arcane laws and vague comments to keep the people he protected exactly where he wanted them.

Everyone hid behind Phillips, and that was the tool he would use now. No matter what happened in the past or the future, he was the impenetrable wall that separated them from risk or injury. Their confidence in him would let him get away with anything, just as it had over the years, because they never saw the man behind the badge. Maggie was his only refuge, and she sure wouldn't want to know about the knife. He knew the look that would cross her face would be the same one as last night when he was still trembling over Joe, which was just like the time he drowned the tourist she said had assaulted her.

"You're my little hero," she'd said, as she unlaced his wet boots and helped him out of his waterlogged clothes.

"It was terrible."

"You had to do it. What was it like? Did he make gurgling sounds? Were there lots of air bubbles?"

She slowly got him naked, dried his chest and arms, and then got on her knees in front of him. As she closed in she glanced up and smiled, looking as frightening as she did sexy.

"Don't, Maggie. Please."

She kept licking and sucking until he had little choice but to give her the sex she needed, and receive the pleasure she seemed intent on giving.

No, there was definitely no point in worrying Maggie about the missing knife, so he locked up the note and looked for all possible motives Stewart could have for making a trade. His best guess was that he wanted to save Jennifer and make himself look like a hero to her. He'd probably learned enough in the military police to bust a lock, so how hard was it for him to get the knife? He had a little more guts than Phillips expected, but he could use that against him, especially his courage to meet him at midnight.

Two people had died in Buxton already. When Phillips solved the murders and put his people at peace, he would be a hero, even if – especially if – he had to kill two people in the process. The town might even name a park or marina after him, or nominate him for *Parade Magazine's* Law Enforcement Officer of the Year.

It was this silver lining that Phillips chose to see. Stewart had probably witnessed him murdering Joe, the knife he used was missing, and his career looked in jeopardy. But if he stayed cool and didn't panic he could turn it all around.

He would kill Stewart first. There was no other way, unless he killed Jennifer first and hid her body. No, her body couldn't be moved because the state police would be drawn in by then, so her body had to be found where she died. So yes, he was right the first time, Stewart had to die first.

The meeting was all set, so it would happen tonight. The skeleton of Captain Dave's washed-away house would be perfect. He couldn't have picked a better place himself.

Of course he would have to worry about a trap. He clearly wasn't the only guy in town who could set people up, so he had to make sure no one showed early to rig up cameras or microphones.

Just then his deputy came in with a dollop of blue cheese in the corner of his mouth, odd evidence that it was still daytime when it seemed much later because of the dark sky.

"Really blowing out there, Sheriff. Town is pretty well boarded up though. Weatherman says it'll hit about between eleven and the early morning hours. The worst of it, that is."

"I want you on surveillance until then."

"Surveillance? Where?"

"Hide in the dunes by Captain Dave's old house. The one torn apart by last year's nor'easter."

"Hide in the dunes? And see what? It's blowing the fur off animals out there, and in the dark I won't see nothing but –"

"I'm meeting the man who killed Lenny and Joe out there at midnight. On the driveway in front of the house. Pick a good spot and use your radio to keep me posted throughout the evening about who's on the beach, in the dunes, around the house, or on the road. I want to know everything. This will be your chance to be a hero, son."

"Yeah? How's that?"

"We're dealing with an extremely dangerous criminal the whole state is writing about. You and me are going to tag him tonight and…well, I'm a little embarrassed to say it, but I'm scared that I can't do it without your help."

The deputy was excited until the sheriff said he was scared. "What am I going to do?"

"You ate, right?"

"Just did."

"Take some candy bars and water and go find a place now. Don't be obvious about it and for God's sake don't park your patrol car anywhere near there. In fact, get your stuff together and I'll drop you off on my way home to board up my house."

"What else should I take?"

"Rain gear, binoculars, and that scoped rifle in the rack."

"Scoped rifle? Scope won't do no good in the dark."

"When the time comes, I'll shine a flashlight at the guy, so just shoot where I point. Get some sightings in this afternoon while there's still a little light. Get your distance right so you'll be ready."

166

The deputy walked slowly to the gun rack and opened it with the key. He looked uncertain as he pulled down the rifle.

"Maybe we should get more help, Sheriff. I ain't scared, but I sure don't want my face skinned off. There's only two of us."

"And one of them. Maybe two."

"Two?" He put the rifle back. "Sheriff, this is crazy."

"I won't let you get killed."

"It's my birthday next week. Mary Ellen's throwing me a party in Nag's Head."

"And I'll be there to help you celebrate. Come on, get your stuff and let's go."

11

Stewart took Jennifer back to his house after getting her got out of jail. Neither spoke as the radio declared the lowest prices of the year on new Chevy trucks, followed by a hurricane update from NOAA's Weather Center that urged residents of low-lying areas and barrier islands to evacuate immediately.

He turned off the radio in order to have a clean break between the end of strategizing and the beginning of action. If any time was left after telling her his plans for tonight, he would see if she shared any part of his crazy idea about trying a future together. Making plans for *after* a life-threatening mission was his way of dealing with the fear that preceded it, so if he could look beyond tonight and see a future with him in it, he would trust that vision as an omen that he would live to see it come true.

It was nice to put Jennifer in those plans, but it was tricky, too, because it meant they both needed to stay alive. Yet she still had no idea that he'd had no choice but to give Phun a perfect chance to kill him, or that for his plan to work she would come very close to getting killed too. He had more than enough reason to be scared for them both.

He couldn't remember ever facing a fight where he was so outmatched that chance favored his enemy, but it was the only way to wrap Phun's death up with Lenny's and Joe's, and that was absolutely essential. So to better his odds he needed Jennifer's help.

She sat beside him and shared the silence, even prettier than the day they'd met because now he knew her a little, and he liked what he knew. She'd watched as he switched off the radio, and then her eyes followed his hand back to the steering wheel. She'd glanced at him and bit her lip and then turned away, all signals that she wanted to talk. She'd been quiet since their discussion about the knife he'd stolen, and silence was unusual behavior for her. Since she was professional enough not to jeopardize a mission by acting unusual that meant her silence was a genuine reflection of some true feelings.

People in the intelligence community had pretty much the same varieties of personalities as in any line of work, and the best of them adapted theirs to the job at hand. Stewart was a quiet man whose success capitalized on the fact that he was plain vanilla and never attracted much attention, whereas Jennifer used her charm and outgoing personality to win the string of successes that had brought her to Buxton.

But that contrast between them was mainly just the performance that took place in front of everyone. Offstage they were amazingly similar in the way they built settings and changed characters. In the subtle efficiency with which they both killed, they seemed to be identical.

She wasn't trying to charm or manipulate him now, though. She'd said she was sorry and it sounded sincere. Reinforced by the nervous nibbling of her fingertips, it was a good indication that things were getting personal. Of course, it could just be confused feelings over her brother, but Stewart wanted to believe that Jennifer was thinking of him. Never before had Stewart known another spy who, like him, hid so much so deeply because of the odds of being hurt or exploited. It felt special to him and probably special to Jennifer too.

The rain started suddenly as they rode to his house, driven into the island with the fierce winds that were jangling streetlights and shredding awnings. They only saw a few other cars on the road, which meant that everyone else had either evacuated the island or was hunkered down to ride out the storm.

He parked under his house, in-between the stilts that elevated the main floor above the ground. He grabbed his pack from the backseat and held her door open, then they dashed up the steps that were open to the weather, getting soaked in the few seconds it took.

"Ever seen it rain so hard?" he asked after they got inside and he gave her a towel.

She shook her head no as she dried her face.

"I'm going to change. Be right back."

He went into his bedroom, dried off quickly and changed into dry clothes. He stuck the backpack with all his gear under some dirty clothes in his closet, careful to make sure some of the pack was showing.

He opened the bedroom door quietly and watched Jennifer walk around his house, looking at everything with an appraiser's eye. She was out of her clothes and wrapped in the towel, and as he watched he chose to believe she was sizing up his home to see how well it fit.

"Your home is very nice," she said when she noticed him.

"Comfortable."

She walked into the kitchen, separated by a counter from the living room. "You should have shown me something like this. It's exactly what I was looking for."

"Was? You mean our local constable has given you doubts about living here?"

"No." She straightened a painting he'd bought at the grocery store, and then turned to face him. "Your setting me up gave me doubts about living here."

"No reason to blame the town then. It's a good place. I'm just one person."

She ran her hand along the countertop as she walked toward him. "Are you?"

The startling direct question. Except this time Stewart didn't feel threatened by it. In fact, he was glad she'd finally asked. "Pardon me?"

She stopped three feet away and looked him straight in the eyes. "Are you just one person?"

He felt like blurting out that he was the man who didn't really exist, the ghost she'd come to find. He was winding down a career of secrecy and could afford to say it, especially since she had a right to know and a clearance that justified it. It would be shoptalk and nothing more, a chance for both of them to find some relief in the truth, and a chance to slip in that he was also a good and decent man looking for peace.

Simone, God love her, had never asked, and he'd often wondered how different his life might have been if she had. Would he have lied back then? Probably, but at least he would have thought about telling the truth, the same way he was thinking about giving Jennifer the truth now.

To hell with it, he would focus on a future with Jennifer instead of a future alone because it was just too marvelous a feeling, and that future could almost start right away. The first step was forcing out the impossible words.

"A shrink might argue that I've got a couple of folks inside, but my birth certificate only has one name on it."

"Can I see it?"

She was way outside professional boundaries, which proved it was definitely personal to her too. Damned if that didn't feel great.

"Sure. Tomorrow. It's in a box at the bank."

She smiled. "Tomorrow then."

"Care to take a hot shower? Good pressure."

"That would be nice."

He motioned her into his room. "Help yourself to any dry clothes you find in my closet."

"Thanks."

He heated some milk in a pan for hot cocoa and unwired the phone outlets while he waited, enjoying the fantastic feeling of having her in his home and in his shower. He tried to think about the night's work ahead, but his mind kept thinking of her naked back there in his room, using his things as if they were her own. He ached a little for her, and it felt great to know he still could. He didn't know much about love, if that's what the feeling might become some day, but he knew it was an elusive and special gift to be treasured.

The rain hammered his house as he stirred Jennifer's cocoa, replaying their talk in Phillips's jail about making love. She was kidding in conspiracy with the way he'd teased her, but underneath all that she seemed to want him, plucking the strings of how nice it felt to be cared about.

But he could not let those good feelings distract him too much or he might not live to act on them. Phun was still out there. He'd checked out of his hotel, but his rental car company said the car hadn't been returned. He might have abandoned it, but Stewart felt sure he would stay until he found and killed Cruiser.

The only reason Stewart was still alive was because Phun only knew the CIA's lies about his being black that had been disseminated since his first hostile country mission in Angola when he'd run the operation on Jonas Savimbi. Cruiser performed so well that even after Congress cut funding Langley ran his operation off the books until support was legalized again.

It was only logical to assume a success in that part of the world meant Cruiser was black, and Nick got everyone to believe it. Cruiser was commended by William Colby but refused to go to Langley, establishing a pattern that seldom varied, and never without a cover. Now hardly anyone suspected Cruiser wasn't black, making him a ghost of an agent living a lonely and thrilling life that denied him a family while sumptuously feeding the lie that he wasn't really running, all the while providing a steady fix of the high-octane adrenaline to which he'd long been addicted.

He'd joined the Company for a few years of adventure, which was easy enough to understand of a young man. But why had he stayed so many years longer than he'd originally intended? Only in past months had the undeniable truth stamped itself so indelibly on his passport: he had never quit chasing assignments because he'd never stopped running away. Running was the last thing he would ever have expected to discover about himself, whereas the accompanying loneliness was something he understood fully.

But it was precisely that lonely image that protected him from the low-level clerks and assistants most often responsible for security breeches, the very ones Nick suspected of revealing Stewart's whereabouts to Phun. Whenever he met a support person in a target country he automatically laid plans to recruit them, learning whatever he could about them, most importantly their flaws.

Sometimes the recruit was just a loner who needed a friend. Sometimes they needed money, and Cruiser would get them addicted to an income stream from innocent side work that had nothing to do with their real job. As their dependency on Cruiser grew, the recruit had fewer ways to say no when Cruiser casually asked the occasional question that crossed slightly over the line of secrecy. Once the first small secret was exposed – which he called the first olive out of the jar – the rest came easier.

There was never a shortage of good recruits, even in small towns like Buxton. There was the rare but occasional disaffected patriot, but most often they were just men and women whose self-perception was grander than whatever recognition they'd received during bland careers with few or no highlights.

Jennifer came out of his bedroom wearing one of his sweaters, toweling her hair as if re-enacting that same life-changing moment of his time with Simone. Jennifer was so short that his sweater came down to her knees and looked both modest and sexy. He was overwhelmed by the replay of a beautiful woman toweling her wet hair while he held the hot drink he'd made for her. It was an amazing feeling, but the evening's bloody finale required his complete concentration and there was very little time left.

As if to prove the point, the hurricane suddenly shook his home and bent the glass of his windows. Since he hadn't boarded them up he could only hope the hurricane kept to its predicted path and made landfall a little farther north. If it hit much closer he would probably lose his home.

While Jennifer sipped the cocoa he built a fire, hoping to create a sense of calm that should make things easier. As the kindling burned and ignited larger pieces, Stewart appreciated the warmth and peace, and the amazing fact that he wasn't alone. He poked the wood benignly, wanting the fire to feel disarming to Jennifer. She was his very last recruit on this mission, and to keep her from hating him later he needed this to seem like her idea, a decision made freely based upon the truth she should have just learned in his bedroom. The fire would help.

If she didn't help him the fire might be the last one of his life. He'd been honest with himself and accepted that Phun was the superior fighter in the very arena Stewart had designed for their battle. Maybe things would be different if he was still thirty, or even mid-forties. But even with a lifetime of training and the intense level of fitness he demanded of himself, he now had to factor in age, which he'd never done before.

As Jennifer sat on the floor beside him, Stewart wished he'd ignored his mistrust of easy solutions that might leave his fingerprints. He could have easily staged something less complicated, perhaps taunting Phun into attacking his house and then shooting him as an intruder. He'd been foolish to be so complex with so dangerous an enemy, and foolishness killed more of his kind than all enemies combined.

He would know soon enough if his determination to hide behind a maze of misdirection would prove a deadly devotion to his reputation. If he'd complicated the game just slightly beyond the realm of possibility, it was too late now to change. Phun needed to die tonight, and with Jennifer's help it was still possible for his death to remain completely unconnected to him or The Agency.

With the fire warming him, Jennifer sitting beside him, and Phun's threat looming just ahead of him, he really wished he'd succeeded in China. But no one could have gotten to Phun because he was too well insulated. He never even thought the bomb would kill him because nothing – people, food or packages – got near Phun without a thorough search. Cruiser's best hope back then was that sending in the bomb would anger Phun enough to expose himself. Cruiser never thought the bomb might kill his family.

Stewart carried guilt for the deaths of Phun's wife and kids, and remembered them the same way he remembered the doctor in Nicaragua: innocent people who willingly chose to be in the wrong place. They knew the risks of allying themselves with people who attracted violence, but even so their deaths were mistakes he regretted, especially since the aunt of Phun's small children sat curled up beside him.

Jennifer stared at the fire and sipped her cocoa, but still hadn't said anything.

"Warming up?"

"Sorry I look scruffy."

"You don't look scruffy at all. But speaking of looks, I saw someone today who reminded me of you."

She kept staring at the fire.

"Didn't you say it was your brother who suggested you buy a house in Buxton?"

"Yes."

"Do you think it's possible he's here?"

"I...I'm not sure. He said he might fly over from England to see me, but I haven't heard from him."

"Maybe he called your motel while you were in jail. You might want to check."

"I suppose. Why?"

Stewart poked the fire and put on some larger logs. Part of him wanted to forget the whole thing and let someone else deal with Phun. Nothing Phun knew about Cruiser was true, so Stewart could live out his life in safe anonymity – jeez, at this point he'd be happy to live at all. Why did he have to deal with that animal?

"If he were here, I could use a hand."

"Really? With what?"

"We know the sheriff killed Joe, and probably Lenny. But the town loves him, so if your brother were here, maybe he could act like a witness when I confront the sheriff about it."

"Why on earth would you do that?"

"Who else is there? I got some law enforcement training in the army. Remember me telling you that?"

She raised one of her eyebrows.

"But the state police aren't going to take me seriously when I accuse a second-generation lawman of murder, at least not unless I have evidence or a confession. There's the knife, but I'm not sure it can be tied to Phillips. I need a witness when he admits to murder, if I can get him to say it in exchange for the knife."

"Didn't you get it out of his trunk?"

"Yes, but it's my word against his. Nothing to prove that's where it came from."

She got up and paced. The house creaked from the wind that battered the windows.

"Okay, I'll call my motel for messages."

"Think he'd help me?"

"I don't know. He wouldn't be afraid, but I don't know if he'd want to get involved."

"I understand that." Stewart prodded the fire as he chose his next words carefully. He didn't want them to sound like blackmail, although that's exactly what they were.

"Would it help if you told him you're a suspect in Lenny's murder? Phillips has to pin the deaths on someone, and he's already done a good job of making you look like the killer."

"With your help, I might add."

"It was dumb of me to plant the knife in your car. But nevertheless, you are a suspect. And innocent."

"Let's see if he's even here."

"Help yourself. I didn't see your cell phone."

"The sheriff took me out of my motel room without it." She went to the kitchen but came right back.

"The phones are dead. The storm, I guess."

"You want to use my Jeep?"

She kept trying to figure him out, but he'd set her back too many steps.

"I suppose."

"If he's here and willing to help, ask him to meet me at the municipal boat ramp at eleven-thirty tonight. Do you know it?"

"It's where Lenny was killed."

"Figured you'd remember. Can you give him directions?"

"It shouldn't be a problem, but like I said, I'm not sure he's even here."

"I hope he is. I'd hate to ask you to be the witness, especially in this storm." He laughed. "Not that you aren't pretty when you're soaking wet."

She looked confused and then touched her hair.

"I'll be back in two hours. Eight at the latest, okay?"

"Wear this." He pulled a foul weather jacket out of the closet.

* * *

Jennifer slipped and fell as she ran down the steps. The rain quickly soaked her in spite of the jacket, but she didn't mind because things were going to work out for her after all. Without his even realizing it, Stewart had created a way for her to accomplish her mission simply by telling Phun that *Stewart* was actually Cruiser, the man who murdered his family. When Phun went after him, Cruiser would kill him for her.

She'd flip-flopped about her feelings for Phun until she ended up feeling nothing but sadness for him. Now Stewart would be the one to do the execution, and her relief overpowered all the humiliation of being used and manipulated. Hell, Stewart was none other than Cruiser and there was no one better in the trade, so of course he'd been able to control her. She had nothing to be ashamed about.

And now she was driving his Jeep and wearing his sweater and jacket. She felt stupid that it took her so long to figure it out, but no one could blame her because Cruiser had hidden behind such a clever disguise. It was genius for Jay Stewart to convince the entire intelligence community and all of his enemies that he was a stocky black man, and although she'd always doubted Stewart's alleged background in the Army, she never seriously questioned his backstory until they'd gone to his home.

That's where she discovered that the white real estate agent who looked more like a professor than a killer was actually the man she'd studied the way a groupie obsesses over her favorite rock band. She had actually been in his

179

bedroom. He had built her a fire and made her hot cocoa. CIA Agent Cruiser, a man whose feats were respected worldwide, especially by his enemies.

When she'd gone into his closet for something to wear, she'd seen his small backpack stuck under some dirty clothes as if he'd hidden it quickly. Sure, it was possible that a private investigator or military policeman might have those kinds of items, but her instincts said that the Russian night scope, Czech knife, Chinese transmitter and half a dozen other items from around the world belonged to Cruiser.

He had so deadly a reputation that she actually tingled for having been near him. She'd heard about his days in Angola and Rhodesia, and that he'd personally killed over twenty people in military operations and at least half again that number in clean and surgical coups and assassinations. He'd even been left for dead once by a local cadre in Tanzania, where he was staging an overthrow of Uganda's Idi Amin Dada.

That event was taught at MI6 as a model for protecting secrets because Cruiser's cadre of rebels had scattered as they were overrun by soldiers, leaving Cruiser to destroy the documents that would incriminate America. He was shot in the chest, but even then, bleeding and half unconscious, he'd killed both soldiers who'd attacked the hut, and finished his shredding.

After that, the CIA floundered about supporting his attempt to oust Dada, but Cruiser ignored their reluctance and worked it alone. That on-the-spot decision was an amazingly bold move that only added to his legend. It defined his career, especially after his decision found political support in Washington.

And now she was driving his car.

Her ego was no longer bruised from him setting her up with Sheriff Phillips or staging the fight with Joe. She wasn't a match for Cruiser and would never pretend to be. It had been an important battle when she thought he was just a realtor with a quick mind, but things were suddenly different and that enabled her to be honest about being intrigued by Stewart from the start, even before he risked his own arrest to get her out of jail.

Then he admitted to liking her when they drove to his house, and now he turned out to be Cruiser, a man she'd admired since first hearing about him at sniper school when an instructor had spoken with reverence about a whack job he'd done with an incredible agent named Cruiser, a man with whom he'd worked very closely, yet had somehow never met.

Cruiser would definitely be able to kill her brother. He was clearly the superior warrior. She could pit Phun against Cruiser and Phun would die. Regardless of Phun's training and numerous victories, Cruiser was invincible, or nearly so. It would take more than one man like Phun to kill him.

She did want to talk to Phun before he died, though, and in the honesty of the moment she hoped to catch that playful tone he used when they were kids, reinforcing her memory of the way he was before he turned vicious. It would be a nice memory to have after he died.

It wasn't until she was in Stewart's shower that she finally understood that her pity for Phun didn't mean she wanted him to live and continue threatening her country. It merely meant that she no longer wanted to be the one to kill him. Her conscience could support her acting as an accessory to his death far easier than the cause of it. Meeting her in Buxton must have been a distraction for him, and she would use that by offering to serve up the

181

legendary Cruiser without giving any clue that winning was something Phun had no chance of doing.

She sped through the boarded-up town looking for Phun's Impala along the deserted streets, sure he hadn't changed it because he would use it to test her, trusting her not to give him up while at the same time defying her to come after him. It was almost impossible to see as rain hammered the Jeep and rendered the wipers nearly useless. Flooded streets were swept over by waves as the hurricane bullied its way across the island and into the sound.

She drove down each street that went to the ocean. At the dead ends of those streets she could just barely see the ocean boiling with whitecaps as big as houses and probably taller. She was positive Phun would be out there somewhere because he craved any experience to witness power, as though he always wanted to learn something new about overwhelming force. He was probably out on the beach taking the kind of beating that, even as a child learning martial arts, he seemed to pride himself in enduring.

His car was the only one in the parking lot of Joe's fishing pier. Sand and brown sea foam piled up against it and made it look derelict. If left overnight it would probably be destroyed by the storm. She forced her door open and climbed out into the violence of the hurricane.

There were big metal gates under the sign that said, "Best Ocean Fishing on Hatteras Island," but the gates weren't locked. The wind pushed them away from the railing and then slammed them back so hard the noise made her jump as the wind tore at her clothes. Cold water ran down her back and made her shiver as she fought for each and every step.

Her brother was standing at the far end of the pier but she was afraid to go to him because the pier was buckling in the storm, groaning and scraping as the fierce Atlantic tried to tear it into pieces small enough to eat.

Waves broke underneath and shot water like geysers between the planking, and as she looked toward the end, a wall of dark seawater broke from one side of the pier to the other and tried to wash Phun away. At one point a wave loomed up and then broke directly over him. He'd glanced back for a second and seemed to see her as the wave covered everything for several seconds and knocked her down as it swept down the pier toward the parking lot. It sluiced her to the edge with so much power she almost went over, but when the water drained off, Phun was still out there.

She hardly looked at him as she got close, trying to keep her balance as the ocean surged up from below, reaching for her through the gaps from the missing boards. She grabbed him from behind and twisted him around, then shouted into his face. "You came to kill Cruiser, didn't you?"

He looked happy to see her. He put his hands on both of her shoulders and looked her over.

"It's magnificent out here! Look at that power."

Both of them looked at the ocean, inconsequential and helpless children against the monster that lived all around them and grabbed at them from all sides, the waves as threatening, beautiful, and scary as giant warriors dancing around helpless sacrifices. Then a wave knocked her feet out from under her. Phun grabbed her and kept her from going over as the pier shuddered and something else came loose behind them.

183

"Yes," he shouted, but she cupped her ear to show she couldn't hear.

"Yes," he shouted again, while nodding his head. "I came for *Sha Hai Wo Jia de Shung Shou.*"

He suddenly looked weak, as if the words had killed his family all over again and left behind a frail person who'd lost everything. Nothing Jennifer knew about her brother could reconcile his look that pleaded so silently and powerfully for pity. She stepped forward and put her arms around him, hugged him and felt him quiver while the ocean continued its attack on them both. "I'm sorry, Phun."

He had never been pitied in his life, or if he had, she knew he'd never learned what to do with it. He gently pushed her away and stared at her the same way he had after he killed their father. Just like that night, there was confusion and grief on his face, but neither in great quantities, as if his suffering didn't go deep enough to spark redemption.

She moved close enough to make sure he heard her. "Go to the boat ramp where you killed Lenny. Cruiser will be there at eleven-thirty." Then, just to help Cruiser by having Phun show up unarmed, she added, "He won't be carrying a weapon because he thinks he's meeting an ally who'll help him catch the sheriff." She stepped back and turned away while he was still staring at her.

As she looked toward shore and tried to time her escape, a big wave slammed into the middle of the pier and bent it, dragging one side into the ocean and tilting that whole section steeply as the planks stayed bolted to the bent framework that buried itself in the black water below.

She grabbed the opposite handrail and pulled herself over the chasm, knowing that weak spot would be the first part of the pier to vanish. Her feet dangled over the sunken boards that washed around in the water below, but she kept a tight grip as she went hand over hand to safety. She got to the gates and looked back to see her brother still at the end, his hands held up high in defiance of whatever life threw at him.

She knew it was just her imagination, but she could swear she heard him screaming.

12

Stewart didn't want Jennifer back in his home, and not just because there wasn't time. The final act had started and events would be happening with a quick precision. Yet his determination to keep her out had as much to do with his feelings as his timeline, so when she pulled into his driveway he ran out the door to take her to her car. He jumped in as she climbed to the passenger seat.

"Did you find your brother?"

"God, it's really storming. Yes, he'll meet you at the ramp at eleven-thirty. He'll help you with the sheriff."

"Lucky for me that he's here."

"Suppose so."

"I'll drive you back to your motel. You could stay here but your motel is boarded up and safer. You saw my windows bowing."

"The road is washed over. Watch out for lawn chairs and trash cans."

"I've seen boats pile up on the island during these storms."

"No boats," she said, and then smiled. "I would have noticed."

As he searched for the road he turned on the radio because he didn't want to talk but wanted some noise. Silence could be like darkness – a good place for fear to breed – and he had a belly full already and none of it doing him any good.

Besides, it had all been planned and all been said and all of the moving pieces were now shifting into place. There was nothing to talk about and nothing left to do but finish it, so there was no use being afraid. Fear would get him thinking about the dozens of other professionals Phun had already slaughtered, and while that had been important to consider in the planning stage, it would only cause doubt now that the fight was coming.

The weather service re-broadcast its hurricane warning and a plea for evacuation, and the DJ followed it up with a song about rainy nights. Stewart turned it up and forced the jumps out of his throat enough to sing along, and that made Jennifer smile.

Her motel was dark and the windows were boarded up, but the power was still on because a small *Vacancy* sign was lit up in front of the dark office. The wind blew the rain sideways and they got soaked as they ran up the stairs. He opened the door to her room and they tumbled in, slamming the door before reaching for the lights. Neither spoke until they caught their breath.

"I guess you'll be okay here. If the place starts coming apart, go down a floor and break into another room. Get into the bathtub and cover up with blankets."

"You're going to be careful? I mean, with the sheriff, the weather…lots of things could happen."

"Thanks for talking to your brother." Without realizing it he reached out and touched her arm. He looked at his hand and marveled that he'd done something so unconsciously.

187

Few things felt less unnatural to him than expressing emotions without censor or strategy, but he'd just been spontaneous for the first time in decades and it felt great.

"I'll take you to breakfast in the morning if anything's open."

"The storm will most likely have passed so it will be like a rebirth around here. We'll find somewhere to eat."

"I'd like that, Jay. It'll be my treat."

He reached for the door but didn't open it.

"Look Jennifer, if for some reason I don't show in the morning, you have to know that I wanted to."

It was absolutely the truth, but he felt dishonest saying it. After first deciding to use that line two days ago he'd carefully rehearsed it to make sure it revealed his fear of her brother. Back then, he hadn't really expected to like Jennifer. But since his feelings for her were the only part of his plan that had changed, he still needed her to know he was afraid.

"I expect to see you at breakfast," she said firmly. "I'd like scones and hot tea." Then she cut him a look and smiled. "And we'll find some oatmeal and raisins for you."

He stuck a confused look on his face but felt a whole lot better as he turned the knob and the wind snatched him out of the room. She'd put it all together, thank God. Oatmeal and raisins was Cruiser's trademark breakfast, one of the few truths he'd ever revealed, a curious anomaly of the man so feared worldwide that his reputation seemed to dictate a breakfast of fresh blood and raw arteries. Now there was no way she could resist sneaking down to the boat ramp to get an impossibly rare glimpse of Cruiser at work, and that was exactly where he needed her.

He went home and poked the fire back to life, then added enough logs to make it roar. October was almost too early for a fire, but there was no telling when he'd do this again, or if he ever would. Every once in a while he stepped outside to cool down in the rain, just to keep the hot fire feeling so good.

He tried to meditate, his legs folded and eyes closed, working the tension out of his muscles and body, trying to make himself fluid and ready for what was soon to come. He knew Phun would be doing much the same thing, but with more accuracy and ritual.

As far as Stewart knew, Phun had never lost a fight, regardless of the odds, and as he pictured Phun working his way up from meditation to the murderous movements at which he was so efficient, it seemed less and less likely that Stewart would win tonight. It was terrifying to doubt himself at this apex moment of such a complex struggle, but pure and brutal honesty was a great tool for survival. He hadn't given up on victory but he did accept the odds.

If only Phun wasn't so damn good, or if Sheriff Phillips had been much better, he could have manipulated Phillips into going to the eleven-thirty meeting instead. Phun would have attacked Phillips without hesitation and Phillips could have pulled out his gun and shot Phun, ending the whole bloody business. But Phillips wasn't good enough, not by a long shot.

It was impossible for him to meditate as his house strained against the hurricane, with wind blasting the large glass panels facing the ocean with so much force that it grotesquely distorted the reflected lights. So had he thought of everything? Was the game board completely ready, with every single piece in place? Had any variable been overlooked or poorly considered? Were there contingencies for every contingency, suitable alternate plans if everything went wrong?

I won't let this scare me, for I am ready and prepared.

"Oh, hell," he muttered. "Why couldn't Phun have just *shot* Lenny? Then the sheriff would have just *shot* Joe and I could just go up and *shoot* Phun. Bang, bang, bang, over and done with."

But no, now Stewart had to commit torture, pure and simple, and he'd never tortured anyone before. The idea sickened him, but even in his disgust he checked to make sure the pliers were zippered into his jacket pocket.

He went to the kitchen and paced. He thought about calling for help, but the mission was running on time and everyone had been put in play. If help was coming, it was already on its way. If it wasn't, then he would probably fail.

At ten o'clock he went into the bathroom and shaved off his beard. He was going to meet a mortal enemy tonight, and possibly his maker, so he wanted to look like himself – at least the rendition constructed by the Puerto Rican doctors after the plane crash.

With the beard gone he managed to find some of his old face in the contours of the mirror's image. It wasn't really that far off the looks of his youth. The scars had healed long ago where the orbits of his eyes had shattered, and his jaw had reset well enough. He popped out the tinted contacts, parted his hair the way he used to, and looked at the real him for the first time since long before China. He ran his hand over the cheeks of his clean-shaven face and said, "Harder for Phun to slice these babies off without a beard to grab," and then forced himself to laugh.

The boat ramp was only ten minutes away, even in such lousy weather, and there was no reason to be early. But the waiting was making him nervous, and nerves were an enemy, too. So Stewart looked for odd little jobs to do around his house. He was half-hearted about it but had an

190

hour to kill and a mind he wanted to distract from worrying.

He wiped off the shelves by the fireplace, then went to his closet and opened a box he'd kept in storage for so long he'd forgotten most of what was in it except for some photos he wanted displayed. This was the first home he'd ever owned, and if he died tonight he didn't want loved ones coming in and not finding their picture somewhere.

On top, in a frame he'd bought in an Egyptian bazaar, was a photo of Simone walking out of the fromagerie in their neighborhood in Paris. She hated the picture, but he cherished it because her eyes said she loved him dearly, and her posture showed how comfortable she was around him.

The photo and the emotions that swirled around it left no doubt that Jennifer had put him on the same emotional road that had led briefly to happiness in Paris. He hadn't stayed on that road with Simone, so where it might take him would remain a mystery until he found the guts to travel it farther.

He dug a little deeper and found a photo of when he was nine, standing with his sister and parents in front of the family Buick on Easter Sunday. His little sister smiled with a missing tooth as she held a big, stuffed bunny in her arms while he held both their Easter baskets.

He loved that picture because it showed him doing the kind of thing he would later do for a living, yet not since that photo had he ever been caught so easily. When the camera snapped, it captured him slipping candy from his own basket into his sister's. As far as he knew she hadn't noticed, and their parents had never said anything, but because he knew what he'd been doing he considered himself caught.

That photo proved how easy it was to be exposed in a deception, and had influenced his entire career as a spy, making him determined to never again be noticed working. He didn't want people to know anything he did, and the photo had taught how hard that would be.

As he polished the glass he admired how his father wore his hat cocked over his eyes like in his Army photos, and the folds in his mother's full skirt that she used to spend hours ironing. But he liked seeing his hand the most, half hidden behind his own basket as he did what no one else ever noticed.

He suddenly realized he'd lost track of time and shook himself back to the present with a new strength and inner peace, relieved when he looked at the clock and saw that thirty minutes had elapsed in those two memories. It was just after eleven.

He reached to the bottom of the box and dug out his Marine Corps dog tags. With both pride and precision he hung them around his neck and pressed them against his chest. If he died tonight he wanted to be properly identified because he'd pretended to be so many people that even he got confused sometimes, living a life no one knew or could ever imagine, burning through dozens of aliases and hundreds of covers, traveling under all kinds of pretenses to do the work people only thought happened in movies.

Pure and absolute anonymity was his safest refuge and closest ally, every bit as reliable as it was false, so he didn't want to chance some clerk from Langley getting his name wrong on the death certificate, and didn't want to go to Heaven under an alias. God probably wouldn't find it funny.

Of course, it might be an advantage if the *Afterlife Express* took him down instead of up. He wondered if there was a way to play the devil and win, and decided there probably was. Everyone could be played. It was just a matter of making the game complex enough to misdirect everyone involved. He'd perfected his sleight of hand performances that depended on people seeing whatever he wanted them to see, and although he just might be good enough to beat the devil, he hoped he wouldn't have to find out.

He stayed in his jeans because they would be hard to grab if he ended up, as he hoped, on the ground with Phun. He didn't wear a shirt, but put on a rain jacket he could take off just before the fight. He knew Phun would be bare-chested, too, because no one who fought for their life empty handed ever wore a shirt that could become an enemy's handhold. Since Jennifer would want to witness a glorious battle, he figured she'd said something to Phun so he wouldn't worry about being shot from a distance. That would allow him the close-in battle he wanted.

He closed the fireplace grate and put the cups in the dishwasher so the house would be neat for whoever came in next, hopefully him. He locked the door and left the key on a nail under the deck, then ran through the stinging rain to his Jeep. He checked the gas, even though he'd filled it earlier. Little things could screw up big plans, so he never took anything for granted.

He drove past the turn-in to the boat ramp. He hadn't missed it, but he couldn't quite make his hands turn the wheel as he thought about all the photos of Phun's victims he'd seen over the years. As much as he tried to block those memories, he couldn't, which was why Phun disseminated them so widely. They were weapons of intimidation, a history of torture that made Phun's enemies approach him with fear instead of confidence, which meant Phun started off already winning.

It worked too, forcing Stewart to drive past the ramp because he couldn't fight Phun without absolute commitment and total belief in his ability to win. Anything short of that with a man like Phun, he might as well save the gas, pull to the side of the road, and slice off his own face.

He drove a hundred yards but had to stop because the remains of Captain Dave's driveway were only a quarter mile ahead. The last bad storm had eroded away the sand beneath it and taken most of the house to sea, leaving a chasm of twenty feet between the end of the drive and the pilings that remained. Sheriff Phillips might already be there, and Stewart couldn't allow his Jeep to be seen early.

That brief thought about meeting Phillips helped him see a future with him in it, and that gave him a boost of confidence for his fight with Phun. So he turned around and passed the boat ramp again, heading back toward town and looking for his turn.

It was just short of eleven-twenty. He was ready and no longer afraid, anxious now and powered by the same force that powered Phun. They were equal warriors with equal causes, but they were playing Stewart's game – at least as far as he knew – and that tilted all advantages in his favor.

He was sure he would get hurt tonight, but he would not die, and the mission he'd failed to accomplish in China would finally be complete. Despite all the attention given to religious extremists, the CIA currently had Phun at the top of their hit list, so in just a few minutes America and the U.K. would be safer with hardly anyone knowing it.

Just past the entrance to the boat ramp an unpaved road went over the dunes and onto the beach. Stewart turned off his lights and followed it as best he could in the rainy darkness. He parked at a low spot between the dunes where his car would stay hidden from anyone passing, assuming the weather ever cleared that much.

He put on surgical gloves and took the knife Sheriff Phillips had used to kill Joe out of the glove compartment. He'd bought one just like it and thrown it away, but kept the sheath and wore it on his belt. He slipped the knife into the sheath. As he opened the car door the wind pulled it away as the rain stung his skin and tried to blind him.

He'd planned to jog to the ramp but couldn't because the wind was too powerful and would have left him too weak. Better to be late and strong than on time and exhausted, but there was a balance in any complex undertaking, a fulcrum on which time and energy teetered precariously. Each second he was late was a second less he could spend fighting, and the whole chain of events was time-critical.

He had classed this as a three-minute fight with a four-minute follow-up. That was his optimum time line, three minutes or less, although he would have preferred a fifteen-second fight. But that was an impossible hope with Phun, and if it went longer than three minutes the balance would shift to Phun because that meant they would be fighting his way. Every second of combat beyond the first one hundred and eighty would take Cruiser closer to death.

Cockle burrs stuck into his bare feet and buried their way in-between his toes, but he ignored them. They weren't even painful really, just annoying, and there would be far too much pain ahead to let them distract him. He knew when to lick his wounds, and this wasn't the time to whine about stickers in his feet.

His jacket was useless, but he had to have it and didn't want to carry it. The hood kept blowing around and

195

covering his face, but he needed to take it off in a hurry when he got near Phun, so he didn't zip it.

When he reached the top of the small dune that separated him from Phun, he dropped to his stomach and crawled through the sea oats. The parking lot was empty except for Phun's car, parked near the water where the flooding tide had swallowed the docks.

Phun was near the ramps, standing there with no shirt or shoes, his arms lifted up to the air while he rotated in each direction as an invitation for his opponent to come out of hiding.

Stewart dropped his head and closed his eyes, reminding himself once more that this was worth it, that his job was to protect the country that Phun threatened. The cold rain made him shiver and he couldn't allow that, so he jumped up and started running toward Phun, needing to heat up his body and throw off the cold that tightened and cramped his muscles.

Phun saw him coming from a hundred yards away. He shielded his eyes against the wind and rain and looked as Cruiser threw aside his raincoat while screaming his way out of the dunes.

Phun screamed too, still trying to get a better look at this white man but not letting that bit of surprise hold him back. He took a defensive position like a combatant expecting an honorable fight in a dojo, his feet apart, his body angled and his hands up.

Cruiser had been stupid to allow his body to cool down because as his bare feet hit the asphalt of the parking lot he stumbled and almost fell. But he managed to pick up speed and get his legs moving in a race with the momentum of his chest.

He was out of control when he got to Phun, but it worked to his advantage by plowing him into his enemy in a wildly unorthodox attack. Phun tried to sidestep and push him past, but Cruiser tangled them together and took him down with Phun's arm wound tightly around Cruiser's neck.

Phun cracked his knee into Cruiser's chin and his elbow against his head as Cruiser reached down and grabbed Phun's ankle, then jerked it sideways while he kept the knee isolated.

Something snapped in Phun's leg but Phun didn't seem to notice. He hit Cruiser so hard and so many times that Cruiser let go of the ankle and Phun jumped up, but immediately fell over. His leg was damaged, but he looked at it like it was a lazy child he could force to obey and then jumped up again, only slightly unsteady.

Cruiser jammed a foot behind Phun's injured knee and then fired his other foot into his groin, sending Phun once again to the ground, but Phun bounced back up as if the parking lot were a trampoline. He stood just out of range, prancing around like he couldn't wait for Cruiser to stand, even as he favored his damaged leg.

As Cruiser shot up from the ground, Phun planted his heel hard into the side of his head, which was the last thing Cruiser expected from a man with an injured knee. The blow rang his ears like he'd been clobbered with an aluminum bat, and he thought his jaw might be broken again.

As he wobbled around, Phun fired his other foot at Cruiser's neck, but Cruiser jinked out of the way and then swept the leg on which Phun was standing. They went down together as Cruiser wound Phun's leg around him like an alligator doing its death roll, bending and twisting and

Wes DeMott

hammering away at the same knee he'd damaged when they'd first hit the ground.

Phun screamed, but it was terrifying for its lack of pain, as if he could vent anger and torment and determination, but not pain. It was the scream of an attacker, not of a man being beaten and certainly not the kind of scream Cruiser was hoping to hear. He continued to twist the leg that now went effortlessly in every direction as though the bones were completely shattered.

He'd confined Phun to the ground so he couldn't use the fierce foot fighting for which he was famous, but now he had to finish it. That meant Cruiser had to face the hands that hammered away on his back, so he let go of the leg and slid up Phun, hugging close so Phun would hit himself nearly as often as he hit Cruiser.

One blow hit the top of Cruiser's head so hard he was sure he heard his skull crack, but when he realized it must have been Phun's fingers shattering he guessed which hand had broken and flopped onto the opposite arm to pin it down. Then he got a grip on Phun's throat and reached down to pull Phillips's knife out of the sheath. One of them would soon win the fight, and so it was time to get to the head of the beast and kill him.

It was a terrible mistake because Phun got his hand out from under Cruiser and rolled away, taking Cruiser with him, forcing the knife out of his hand, leaving Cruiser to claw at the concrete as Phun dragged him to the water, the rain and surgical gloves making it impossible to get a grip as Phun pinned him a foot or more under water.

Cruiser was out of air when he went under, so it was automatic to panic. He fought to control it but he was sucking in water as he fought for air. He looked at Phun through the water that separated them and saw him smile, for just a second, before a small hand with red nail polish suddenly came from behind and snatched back Phun's head.

Phun's grip slipped, and as Cruiser struggled to the surface he saw Jennifer pull Phillips's knife out of Phun's right ear. She shifted the knife to her other gloved hand and plunged it through his left.

Brother and sister hovered above Cruiser for a moment as Phun's eyes rolled back for a last look at her. She let go, and Phun collapsed onto Cruiser, the weight forcing him back underwater until he pushed Phun off and got to the surface.

Cruiser rolled onto his knees and crawled through the water to the dock, which was two feet underwater but a flat place to sit. He was gasping like he'd run a marathon and couldn't make himself stop, couldn't find the breath to power some words to Jennifer. He was unbelievably grateful that she'd shown up, but he didn't like that she really did have to save him. It was a back-up plan he'd hoped not to need, and now he worried how her feelings for him might change because he was less than his reputation.

But he was, after all, human, and that meant there was always someone better or luckier. She'd been around long enough to know that. He thought about trying to prove that no one was invincible by pointing at Phun, but it wouldn't have altered the truth. Phun would have killed him if Jennifer hadn't come to his rescue.

He was too exhausted to speak or turn away when she snatched Phun's hand as if she had to do it before her adrenaline ebbed. In one quick flick she expertly sliced around the bone and then popped off his thumb in the Red Sabbath ritual that had become a warning to unseen enemies, almost as frightening as Phun's face-filleting. As far as he knew, Jennifer was the first woman RS, and although Cruiser wanted the thumb to compound his evidence against Phillips, he knew he would have had better luck arguing with a man about it.

She stood over Phun and looked at his blood clouding the water. Although the wind was still howling, it seemed to be slacking off. Cruiser realized it had stopped raining.

"You killed our father," he barely heard her say, talking mostly to herself. "Didn't you see how much he loved you?"

Her body jerked. He thought she might kick Phun, but she didn't. Instead, she choked back a gasp as if the words had taken away whatever hate she'd had left. She sat at the water's edge and cradled Phun's head in her lap, brushing his black hair from his face. Then she looked at Cruiser as if she'd just noticed him, taking a second to realize that it was his missing beard and contacts that made him look so different.

He coughed out some water and cleared his throat.

She looked at him sadly, then looked at Phun the same way. "I did right, didn't I Jay?"

Cruiser pushed off the dock, splashed through the water to the side of her brother, and put his hand on her shoulder. He breathed deep a couple of times.

"I want to say yes," he said, then sucked in some more air. "But that's for you to decide on your own."

"I know," she said without conviction, and then looked at him sadly. "But I think I only did it for you."

"I understand."

"My dog bit me for no reason."

"I'm sorry. What?"

"After getting my stitches, we took it to its favorite part of the woods, where my father and I cried together before he killed it."

Cruiser looked at her face but she was miles away and years long past, a small girl with her pet dog in China.

"We loved that dog, but it did something vicious so it had to die."

She closed the sad part of the memory and got up, still staring at Phun.

"My father was too wise a man not to follow."

"I wish I'd met him."

She looked at the knife she'd used to kill her brother, and then handed it to Cruiser.

"You'll have to do this if you're going to implicate Phillips. There's no way I could."

"I know."

She stood there looking down at Phun until Cruiser led her far enough away to start distancing themselves from what they'd done by the ritual of after-speak. It was the way people who did this kind of work masked the weight of their jobs, the same way a caring cop might make a joke about a murder victim.

"Hey," he said, less light-hearted than he'd hoped to sound. "What kind of bank do you work in, anyway?"

She did not look toward Phun as she forced a sad smile. "My bank? I suppose it's a bit like your real estate office."

He made himself look confused. "I don't understand."

She blinked then turned and walked slowly along the water's edge until she disappeared into the darkness of the battered beach, the wind blowing her ponytail out to the side.

Cruiser went back to Phun's body, which had drifted into deeper water and jigged face down in the waves. He dragged it back onshore and held the knife to Phun's left cheek, just above the jaw line. He closed his eyes and looked away as he sliced. Then he did the other cheek.

He went back and picked up his jacket, put it on and pulled the hood down tight around his face. He carried the slabs of meat and Phillips's knife in his free hand as he ran down the road to Captain Dave's house, Phun's blood dripping onto the wet pavement but immediately draining away.

13

Cruiser realized that the wind had shifted. The fast-moving hurricane had made landfall somewhere up the coast and was beginning its march across the sound, but anyone who hadn't evacuated was most likely still inside.

That was good, but it wouldn't last long. The power and phone companies would get their trucks on the road to re-establish service as soon as possible, and the residents would be out checking the damage and making their own repairs.

Running toward Captain Dave's old driveway, Cruiser thought about the three men who'd died in Buxton. All of their faces had been sliced off, and all of them were missing thumbs. Forensics might be able to prove that the knife used to kill Joe and Phun was different from the one that killed Lenny, but other than that – and what little evidence the sheriff had on Jennifer – all of the murders would be attributed to Sheriff Phillips if everything worked perfectly.

But things didn't always work perfectly, so that kept Stewart planning and working right up to the end. He'd always figured his odds against Phun at less than fifty-fifty, and he'd been right. Only his move to put Jennifer into play had saved him, letting her discover who he was, knowing it would fuel her desire to be there.

He knew she would help if needed because killing Phun was her mission, too, and she had to know it would be easier in Buxton than China. Besides, if she hadn't helped, she would have never been able to explain to her bosses why she stood by and let Cruiser get killed by the man she was supposed to assassinate.

Getting her assigned to his mission in the first place, even before he left China, had been one of his better plays. Although he'd lost track of Phun's sister when she went into MI6, he'd worked strategically with both of their agencies to get it done. His recommendation that Jennifer work with his replacement carried weight, and suggesting they send her to the States beforehand gave him two necessary tools: she could get Phun where he wanted him at the appropriate time, and she could help kill him. Seeing what she looked like in order to identify her brother turned out to be a bonus.

Would she ever realize that she was never intended to go back to China, that from the first moments of Cruiser's involvement her entire mission and all of her training were always intended to come into play in a tiny town on the Carolina coast? Cruiser doubted it, just as he doubted that Phun had ever suspected that the bomb that killed his family – even though they were never intended to get hurt – and the information Phun got about Cruiser, were both planted for the same reason: to lure him to Buxton where Cruiser, with Jennifer's help, could kill him.

That ability to deceive and manipulate while staying completely invisible was the key to Cruiser's success, and the reason he'd survived so long. Given the time to work out a plan that was complicated enough, he could always make destiny happen wherever it best suited his interests, and could make it all look coincidental.

Perhaps he'd become too good at it. Could he ever shut it down and live a normal life of golf or gardening with a woman he could learn to trust, a woman with whom he could be himself? He remembered the spontaneity of his touching Jennifer earlier, and that encouraged him to believe it was possible to make that kind of thing feel natural, to gradually melt down into something purely human instead of so exhaustingly complex.

He pushed those thoughts aside and stopped near Captain Dave's house. He pulled off the surgical gloves and edged into the scrub trees on the side of the road. He looked all around with a big brick in his stomach because the sheriff's car wasn't there. Something had finally gone wrong. He'd concentrated too much on Phun and not enough on Phillips.

He checked his watch and was surprised that it was still only five to twelve. He couldn't help but doubt the time because it felt like twelve-fifteen or later, that the fight with Phun and the jog down the road must have taken at least that long.

Heck, it felt like he'd been underwater with Phun's hand around his throat for almost that much time, but he needed to trust his watch rather than his body's accelerated sense of time. If it was correct, maybe things hadn't fallen apart after all.

Sure enough, a couple minutes later the sheriff drove by, taking his time yet not looking around the way a lawman should. When he drove past the spot where Cruiser was hiding, Phillips turned away and stared at the ocean on the opposite side in order to keep from tipping off Cruiser that he knew he was there. All of that meant the sheriff had probably placed his goofy deputy in the dunes somewhere to watch, probably with orders from Phillips to shoot Stewart.

The sheriff parked his patrol car on the remains of the driveway and got out. He walked to the edge that dangled over the water and looked down, then walked back to the road and scanned the dunes on the other side.

He looked hard at one spot, and that showed Cruiser where Phillips's deputy was most likely hiding. Cruiser watched the sheriff pace and then stop, then look at his watch and pace some more.

He let him wait so that time would work on his side, hoping to jangle Phillips's nerves enough to make him quick or careless, either of which could be an advantage. He couldn't go up to where he now stood anyway because his timing and positioning had to be perfect.

The wind blew steady out of the west, warmer and a little drier than just an hour ago. It wouldn't be much longer before people were on the roads, and this last act had to be over before then. But the time still wasn't right, so Cruiser waited.

Maybe he should have done it another way, perhaps killing Phun earlier in the day and then leaving his face meat in Phillips's house or office. That could have worked, but the evidence against Phillips would be much more compelling this way. Forensics would prove that Phun was murdered a half-mile away just moments before Phillips was seen in the area by his deputy.

The coroner would establish a time of death for Phun and the deputy would testify that the sheriff was near the murder scene. Even if things went wrong and Cruiser didn't survive this, those facts alone would get suspicion off Jennifer.

At twelve-o-five the sheriff seemed to give up. He made a signal toward the dunes and then got into his car. As he started it up, Cruiser pulled his hood into a tight circle that revealed little more than his eyes and nose, and then ran along a line of shrubs until he was across the street from the driveway.

Phillips backed up and when he did, Cruiser ran up behind him and banged on the trunk lid. Phillips hit his brakes and skidded quickly to a stop. By the time he cracked his door opened Cruiser was already beside the car and blocking the door. Phillips looked up and reached for his gun.

"No need for that, Sheriff," he said quickly, his words racing against Phillips's gun hand. "I'm not armed and didn't mean to scare you. Just running late, that's all. Almost missed you."

Phillips stared through the darkness at what little showed of Cruiser's face.

"Then step away from the car so I can get out."

"Can't. I know you've got a deputy out there and I'm guessing he's ready to shoot. I don't know how good he is with a rifle, but I doubt he'll risk the shot if he thinks he might hit you."

"So what do we do? You just going to stand there and stare at me?"

"No, I've got to get going, so here's the deal. I give back your knife and you find someone else to take the fall. Leave Jennifer out of it. Me, too. I don't care what you did to Joe. Just leave us alone."

"You're wearing a wire."

"You can search me after we agree. If I am, then take it with you. I don't care."

Phillips licked his lips.

"I'll search you now. I'm getting out of the car. Let me see your hands."

"I've got your knife in my left."

"Show it to me. Keep it low and move slow as your granny."

Cruiser extended the knife, handle first, with two fingers pressing against the edges of the blade so as not to leave fingerprints.

"Hand it to me. Then I'll get out and search you. If you're clean, we've got a deal."

"Stay real close so I don't get shot."

Cruiser held the knife close to his body so that no one in the dunes could see what they were doing or even know there was a knife. It probably looked like they were having a conversation or argument. Phillips looked at the knife like it was gold or even more precious. He leaned to get out of the car, and as he did, Cruiser lightly flicked the scraps of Phun's face onto the seat. The wind would cover the sound but just to make sure he shouted in a voice near panic, "Stay close to me!"

"You bet I will," Phillips said casually as he leaned his big frame into Cruiser and gently took the knife. "Just stay calm. Now back away a little. Ain't no reason to be *this* close."

Cruiser took a small step back.

"Take off your coat, Stewart. Let me check for a recorder."

Cruiser unzipped his jacket and held it open, but kept the hood on. If he figured the trajectory right, he was probably concealing the sheriff from anyone in the dunes. At the same time, a shot in his back by a high-powered rifle would go straight through and hit Phillips too.

"Can't quite see," said the sheriff. "Let me get my flashlight to shine on you for a second."

He turned to reach into his car, where he would see the slabs of flesh. As he was about to bend into it, Cruiser asked, "Did you get the photos I sent you from China? I did my best to warn you about all this."

Cruiser untied his hood as Phillips jerked back out of the car. When he pushed it back off his head, Phillips stared like he was seeing Stewart for the first time, surprised by the clean-shaven face with different eyes.

"What the ..."

Phillips kept staring as Cruiser watched the tumblers line up. Then the last tumbler finally locked into place and Phillips looked he'd just heard the click of a mine plunger underfoot.

While he stared at Cruiser his hand with the knife rose slowly, almost like it had a will of its own. His eyes dropped and saw his own hand rising, and then looked up again. The look on his face changed as he raised the knife farther and took the single step that separated them.

Cruiser took a big step back, and then another. When the sheriff slashed at him, he jumped back and fell on the ground, four or five feet from Phillips and in the middle of the road. He stayed on his back so he could see what would happen next.

If he'd bet wrong about the deputy, the sheriff would keep coming with hopes of making Cruiser another murder victim in Buxton, slicing his face and puncturing his ears and taking his thumb as he'd taken Joe's. As tired as Cruiser was from his fight with Phun and his jog down the road, coupled with the tactical advantage he'd had no choice but to give Phillips, there was some chance of his success.

But if he'd bet right, if everything worked perfectly, the entire string of murders would be solved in seconds, wrapped up so neatly that no one would question any of the deaths again. Not Lenny's or Joe's or Phun's. Not even Sheriff Phillips's.

Phillips lurched toward Stewart, the knife that had sliced up Joe and Phun still wet with blood as Phillips bent down and made another slash at Cruiser. Cruiser kicked it away but got nicked in his calf. He could have jumped up and taken the knife and killed Phillips with it, but he couldn't allow any doubt that Phillips was clearly a criminal, an aggressor acting far outside the boundaries of the law.

Phillips made another slash and then another. Cruiser kicked at the knife but did it slow enough for Phillips to catch his foot, making Cruiser look even more at risk than before. He deflected the knife with his other foot while Phillips held his leg for several second and slashed away.

Damn it, nothing happened in the woods behind him. Cruiser had bet wrong and the whole performance had gone to hell in the last act. He had a fight on his hands now, and had to start with Phillips already in control of his foot.

He saw an opening to attack and was just about to strike when the rifle shots rang out, so uniform in their timing that it took his trained ear to know there'd actually been three of them. They hit the sheriff from different angles but all of them traversed his skull.

His body wobbled until he crumbled to his knees and fell forward onto the road as Cruiser rolled out of the way. There were at least three FBI snipers in the dunes behind him, but Cruiser had never looked toward the dunes and was careful now not to give them a look at him. He got on his knees with his back to the shooters and wiped a smear of Phun's blood onto Phillips's pants.

As he ran away he knew the snipers would be training their night scopes back and forth between him and Phillips's lifeless body. Although he was their unidentified informant, he worried they might still shoot him by accident or confusion, so he jumped off the ledge of the driveway to the water-covered beach below, then slogged his way back up the coast to his Jeep, mushing through the high water and scummy foam whipped up by the hurricane.

He'd won. By God he'd actually done what he'd set out so long ago to do, completing a mission of honor that he'd never been able to dodge, no matter how much he might have wanted to. He'd made a lucky guess at the weather and timed the whole thing around it. If he'd waited any longer, the winds would have died down enough for the Bureau to put a helicopter in the air to track him, but as it was, the agents were still immobile. They must have been dropped off, or they'd hid their cars far away. No one traveled the road, so he didn't even have to worry about outrunning the radio.

Even if they did pick him up, he'd done nothing wrong. He'd merely played two roles, both a victim and a knowledgeable informant to Phillips's deputy, a man Cruiser had planned to recruit from his first day in town. He'd only talked to him twice on the phone, but what he'd said the first time had piqued the deputy's interest. Yesterday he'd talked to him again and arranged to leave him a dead drop.

The drop was simple enough, just a few photos Cruiser had taken of Phillips murdering Joe, along with a suggestion to contact the FBI for their help in putting him in jail. He told the deputy to abandon his loyalty to the murdering sheriff and tell the FBI whatever Sheriff Phillips asked him to do.

Cruiser's only fear was that the deputy hadn't cleared the drop, or worse, that he had cleared it but shown the photos to Phillips, who might have convinced him they were fakes. Cruiser had prepared for that scenario by telling the deputy in advance that it didn't matter, that the only down side to telling the FBI would be their involvement in a case that deserved their attention anyway. In the event Phillips was innocent, they would promise not to let Phillips know the real reason they were there, thereby protecting the deputy.

But if Sheriff Phillips performed as planned, and proved his guilt by trying to kill Stewart in front of Captain Dave's house, the deputy would be respected and rewarded for his skillful law enforcement. That's what had motivated him. It certainly wasn't his devotion to duty or the desire to rid Buxton of a killer. The deputy was inspired to help by his need to be recognized and respected beyond his less-than-average ability.

The wind blew Stewart along the water's edge at a good clip, and he got back to where he'd left his Jeep so fast he almost missed the access over the dune. His car was there and there still wasn't anyone on the road. The winds were still too strong to risk a helicopter, especially when the murder suspect was already dead a short ways up the road.

He climbed into his Jeep and bounced along slowly as he approached the highway with his lights out, one of only two killers left in Buxton, not counting the FBI snipers who'd come down for one job and would be gone in a couple of hours.

Two minutes down the road he turned on his lights, and five minutes after that he was home. He walked into his house and appreciated the way it looked and felt. It was finally home, a place where he could soon look forward to spending the rest of his life in peace, free of the problems associated with this town he loved so much.

The embers of the fire were smoldering but still hot. He put on some small logs and then showered. As he bandaged his wounds he had a glass of port, then fell asleep on the couch.

14

His cellphone woke Stewart while it was still dark and he sat up too quickly. Pain grabbed him everywhere as he rose stiffly and walked to the kitchen to search for it.

He glanced out the window at the trees. In the clear moonlight he could see them blowing toward the Atlantic in a steady wind. No longer did they whip around in all directions like last night.

"Hello?"

"I've been calling your house and cell since yesterday afternoon, Cruiser. Where have you been?"

"I guess the towers must have gone down, and good morning to you, Nick. How are you?" He put water in the kettle and put it on to boil.

"I'm fine. No, hell, I'm not fine."

"Any idea what time it is?"

"A little after five. Were you sleeping?"

"Wasn't everybody?"

"You have any idea how many problems you've caused for me up here?"

Stewart scratched his face. It felt funny not having a beard. "How could I have caused you a problem?"

"Damn it you *never* pet a burning dog without telling me. It was *you* who leaked to Phun that he'd find you in North Carolina."

"What?"

"Don't 'what' me, smartass. Did you think I wouldn't dig hard to find out who put my best field officer at risk?"

"I thought it was clever. It got him out of China for the first time in his life."

"But we have no authority to work the Typhoon Sanction here and you know it."

"I didn't. At least no one can prove I did. The only prints I left were on an FBI *Request for Recent Contact* on Ernie Roberts, a bit of misinformation I had the Bureau supply the local sheriff. And I made sure that those fingerprints were badly smudged."

"What does that mean? Ernie Roberts…oh, crap, what have you done?"

"Nothing worth worrying about."

"I've got to testify today at a Senate subcommittee because every agency under the Homeland umbrella went whining that we didn't tell them Phun was here, so I want facts. Don't you air me out on this Cruiser."

"Nothing to tell that isn't already handled. Check with your Foreign Counter Intelligence contact in the Bureau. He'll tell you that three FBI snipers just killed the man who killed Phun."

"Phun's dead?"

"Last I heard."

"Who killed him?"

"Officially?"

"I'd believe Tarot cards first."

"There's a local sheriff here who'll take the rap. I supplied a little evidence to help him into their crosshairs, but he was going down anyway for other murders. I used his deputy to bring in the FBI without involving us."

"What if the sheriff realizes he was set up and tells about your involvement?"

"Not possible. He's the guy the snipers shot."

"What about his deputy?"

"Has no idea who I am."

"Sure?"

"I only talked to him on the phone, except for one time on the street, just to see if he knew it was me. He didn't."

Stewart looked outside. The earliest traces of sunrise were radiating over the horizon, just barely visible.

"Who really killed Phun, Cruiser? Had to be you, right?"

"I didn't kill anyone. No stats for me, Nick." He said *Thank God* under his breath.

"I'll never understand…most of my guys live for stats. So who killed him?"

"Jennifer."

"Who?"

"The English woman from MI6. Don't know her real name. She uses the name Jennifer here. Phun's sister."

"Didn't know he had one."

"Yeah. Neither did I. What were the odds of that happening?"

"High, Cruiser. The odds that the agent you got assigned to kill Phun just happening to be his sister are astronomically high."

"It's a small world."

"It ain't that small."

"Thought you had work to do."

"I do, but just keep in mind that a day's coming when one of your elaborate little games blows up in my face, and I swear to God I'll assign you to a sound room with a set of headphones where you'll listen to other cases being worked by people who *didn't* cross me."

"It won't blow up."

"We'll see. I got to go."

Stewart hung up, but stayed at the window watching the wind blow steady against the trees. It was still dark outside but he knew it would be a rare day. The wind was strong and coming across the island, moving straight off shore where it would hold up the faces of last night's waves.

He finished his coffee as he re-bandaged his cuts and put on his wetsuit, then went out into the half-darkness of first light and treaded down the steps. They were still wet from last night's hurricane, so he carried his surfboard under his right arm and some wax in that same hand, using his left hand to hold the railing. He ached in lots of places from Phun's beating and didn't want to make it worse by tumbling down the stairs.

The leash to his surfboard dragged behind him as he walked down the trail to the beach. He'd paid too much money for his home but had done it gladly because it was at the precise spot where the surf broke best on those rare occasions when it broke big, and this would be one of those occasions.

He'd surfed hundreds of times over the years but he hadn't embraced the sport with the respect and dedication it deserved. Too much work and too many distractions had distorted his focus, but now he was ready.

He heard sirens going by and looked back toward the road. Flashing red lights, probably from an ambulance, bounced off the houses and between the trees, most likely carrying away the remains of the chaos he'd caused last night. That meant the photos had all been taken, the surveillance log verified, and the shooting diagram authenticated. Sheriff Phillips's car would be towed away next, leaving nothing behind to indicate what happened in front of Captain Dave's condemned house. Even the FBI snipers didn't really know, except for the small role they'd played.

The air was cool near the water, but the wind blew warmer air over the dunes and against his back. He couldn't quite see the waves but he heard them pounding like cannons in the darkness, spewing white foam that blasted ahead of the breaking waves and lit up in the morning's early rays.

It was big out there. The waves had been building all the way across the Atlantic, and now they were huge and powerful enough to make deep resonant moans that turned into howls as the tops of the big waves lipped over and stretched for the surface of the ocean, forming a massive aquatic barrel Stewart could see with his eyes closed.

More light seeped onto the beach, and with it came other surfers who migrated to the spot like sea turtles returning to the place of their birth, waddling down in their wetsuits and then standing on the beach and staring. They glanced at Stewart and nodded, not surprised to see someone else there so early.

A few carried their surfboards, but they didn't seem likely to use them. Most came empty handed, looking at the big surf there before searching along the coast for smaller waves that better suited their ability. Big days brought caution to the sport, meaning more time in observation and lots of hard honesty.

As the sun crawled over the horizon, Stewart shielded his eyes and managed to get his first real look at the armies of triple-overhead waves. They had incredibly steep and hollow faces that created massive tubes. It was a terrifying but perfect day for his style of surfing, an ideal chance for some high-compression bottom turns followed by a race for his life into the dubious safety of the green room, the vortex of water that surrounded any surfer lucky enough to ride in it.

He studied the breaks and looked for the cleanest lines to follow, watching for clues about new bottom contours and their effect on the waves. He was only able to guess how hard the offshore winds, charging up the face of the waves, would blow him back and try to keep him from dropping in, but judging from the two-story plumes of spray cascading backward as the waves broke, wind would be a big factor.

He was absolutely intent on the waves. It felt great because he could devote his mind to surfing now.

The three men of Buxton who'd murdered his father were dead.

The look Phillips gave when he finally recognized him made it all worthwhile. That Phillips had died a few seconds later made it a nearly perfect application of the skills the government taught him about dealing with enemies.

But were they really his enemies? That was the troubling question because he wanted no part in killing men who'd merely made a mistake as young boys, even if his father had died as a result. Hell, lots of kids make mistakes, but Phillips hadn't shot his dad just once. That could have been accidental, something none of the boys could have expected as they rooted around for coins. No, it was the second shot in the back of the head that was unforgivable.

It was yesterday, or at least would always seem like it, that Cruiser rushed down the stairs as those boys ran out of the house. His mom called for an ambulance as he held his father, blood pouring out of the two holes and making Cruiser's pajamas stick to him as his dad's life slipped away, the first of many men he would eventually watch die.

After decades of shame for doing nothing about it, any guilt he might now carry for murdering those three men was, if nothing else, a change, and probably justified by the fact that the sheriff was also a murderer.

And what about Lenny and Joe, who most likely had played very small roles in the crime? They were more or less like Phun's wife and kids – unfortunate collateral damage, fairly innocent people with the bad luck or judgment to run with a killer.

It was just over a year ago that Cruiser had seen on the internet that the owner of the local surf shop, a guy who'd sold him wax and boards in his youth, had put it up for sale. Cruiser had written a check for the full asking price with the one condition that the guy stayed on as a well-paid manager.

So now he was ready for a new career. He was done running, finally admitting that the Marines and the CIA had been nothing more than excuses to stay away from the home where he had always known he would have to kill or be killed by Phillips, neither option being very appealing. He wasn't proud of the killing he'd just orchestrated in Buxton, but he wasn't ashamed either. He was, however, home, and it was finally time to step closer to becoming the man he once was. Surfing would take him there.

There might be a few small missions ahead for him, but if he stayed alive for another couple of years he felt pretty sure he would make it back to being Ernie, selling surfboards and wax to young surfers and never, ever risking even the briefest glance back at the horrible things he'd done in his wasted three decades of life.

He was thrilled when Jennifer walked down the beach with two Styrofoam cups of coffee. She handed him one but didn't say anything as she sat with him on his surfboard and stared in awe at the power of the ocean.

There were lots of surfers nearby now, most of them just as quiet and as much in awe, but with far less intention than he had of paddling out. One guy was telling his friends in false bravado, "I just want it remembered that I would've gone out if anyone else had."

The longer Jennifer stayed quiet the more he wondered what she would ask. Had she figured out that he'd had no choice but to blow up her brother's home in order to entice him out of his enclave, that there was no way that anyone, even his sister, would have ever been able to kill him in China?

Did she know that he was the one who leaked the information about where he'd moved when he left China, and that he'd devised the whole plan so he could finish his mission on U.S. soil without causing problems?

Did she hate him for setting her up to kill her brother?

Did she know they shared a painful memory of how it felt to have your father murdered, or that his own father's murder was the reason he'd staged this performance in Buxton of all the strange places?

Did she realize he'd played everyone, including her, to orchestrate the deaths of Lenny, Joe, Phun, and Phillips without anyone knowing he'd done it?

Did she even know for sure that he was the spy she'd come to find? Or had his last look of confusion when she'd mentioned his realty office at the boat ramp managed to create some doubt in her suspicions, perhaps making her wonder again if Cruiser wasn't a black man driving a Mercedes and selling insurance in his retirement, while

Stewart was nothing more than a retired military policeman trying to be a good citizen and solve some murders?

He desperately wanted her to understand him, and her knowing those things was a good first step. But if she didn't figure them out for herself, he wouldn't tell her. It was the way things worked in the trade, and he had no business changing the rules.

In the pain of his heart he knew it was better if she never found out. He, Jennifer, and Phun had abandoned everything to travel thousands of miles to Buxton, each seeking their own revenge for the deaths of people they loved. He knew by the look on her face last night that she'd lost her taste for it, so that meant only Stewart had gotten what he'd come for. That made him the winner and everyone else, including Jennifer, the loser, and nobody liked to lose.

"I'm taking off," she said after several more minutes. "A little too exciting around here for me, I'm afraid."

"Done with your holiday? Heading back to the bank without buying a home?" He looked to see her reaction.

"Some holiday," she repeated, making it sound ironic. "I wouldn't quite call it that. Just my bad timing, I guess."

A surfer ventured to the water's edge with his surfboard. An inside wave crashed thirty yards offshore and his presence in the foreground gave it scale. Everyone gasped and the surfer hurried back.

"Thanks for the coffee."

"Afraid it has to count as our breakfast."

He sipped again and the hot liquid warmed his body. "Jennifer, do you think you'll ever come back here?"

She looked around, up and down the coast and back toward his house over the dune. "I don't know. Doubt it. I

222

actually did like it here at first, but it just doesn't feel right anymore."

He looked back at the ocean. "You know you're welcome to come back, right? I've got an extra room. Perhaps one day it might feel right. Who knows?"

"Are you asking me to come back?"

Her eyes told him everything he needed to know and wanted to see, but he felt just as awkward as the day they met, confused about how to be honest. Years ago he'd discarded any hope of ever being in this wondrous kind of situation, having fully accepted his fate as the Flying Dutchman of relationships, a ghost drifting through people's lives but never touching them. Although Jennifer was tough and hard and making her own way along the lonely path he'd traveled for years, he *had* touched her, and in those beautiful brown eyes he could see how hard he'd done it.

She'd touched him too. At first she was just a reminder of his love for Simone, which felt very nice, but as they spent time together his feelings became unique to the two of them and not merely a transference from the past, and that felt fantastic.

Sitting beside her, he realized how big an emotional problem he'd created for himself last night by focusing on a future in order to have confidence for the fight, because the future he'd chosen to see had Jennifer squarely in the middle of it. He loved the fantasy so much that he didn't want to let it go, or ever forget how good it felt. Especially if he ended up living the rest of his life in the ruins of what might have been between them. Both thoughts – having her or losing her – made him ache.

"Sure," he finally said. "Please come back. I'd like that a lot."

"It would be worth it just to find out what happened here. I feel like I was a prop in some magic trick."

"What do you mean? The knife I planted in your car? I said it was a mistake."

"Not that. Just…just idle mumbling, that's all."

She stood and he did too. She held out her hand and waited for him to shake it, but instead he took a step forward and put his hands beside her. He didn't touch her, though, as unsure as a young boy about how to handle this but wanting to show how he truly felt, stymied that those feelings had atrophied like useless muscles ignored for too long.

So he just stood there, awkwardly determined to find a way and just about deciding to kiss her when she stepped into him and pushed herself against his chest. Her arms went around him and held on until his did the same, as if this had been coming since the second they'd met at the house for sale, something they had both wanted to discover and treasure briefly, fully aware it would then be lost again. A couple of surfers hooted nearby but it didn't break them apart.

When he finally let go she looked away before he saw her eyes. She stared at the ocean, and when she looked back she was crying a little. There was so much written on her face, but he was surprised to realize he couldn't read any of it.

Maybe everything she wanted to say was camouflaged by her training, or maybe some past hurt. Maybe he was naïve or stupid about a woman's true feelings. Was she waiting for him to ask her to stay? He was miles away from certain but seemed to be getting that signal from her. He liked the way it felt and was searching for words that just didn't seem to be in his vocabulary.

"Bye," she said suddenly as she turned to walk away.

"But…good-bye, Jennifer. Please be careful. It's dangerous …"

She stopped when his voice cracked. He wanted her to know the truth, but there was just too much of it, and where would he start anyway? He desperately wanted her to know him, and know the horrible price of being alone for a lifetime. He wanted her to stay with him but didn't want to ask anymore than he already had because it had to be her decision. He also wanted to warn her about their profession, telling her so many things she would have to live without if she decided to stay a spy.

"It's dangerous traveling the two-lane road back to Manteo," he said, sadly aware that he'd trained himself too well to say any of it. "Watch the oncoming traffic."

She smiled weakly and took five slow steps, the sand barely kicking up off her bare heels. Then she stopped and turned back around.

"Be honest with me. Please. You're not really Jay Stewart, are you?"

He was glad for the direct question. She'd hinted her suspicion last night, but subtle hints had never deserved honest answers. If Simone had asked directly, there was a small chance that things might have been different between them, and different for him now. Jennifer had made a big step, so he was going to tell her the truth. He knew too well the cost of lying.

"You're right. I'm not Jay Stewart. To be honest, I have no idea if there really is such a person."

She smiled as if laughing at her own stupidity, embarrassed that it had taken her so long to be sure, and even then she had to ask.

"Ernie," he said as she continued to stare, his real name an unfamiliar and foreign secret he had never intended to share again. "Ernie Roberts," he forced himself to say again, loud enough that a couple of other surfers turned at the name. "How did you know?"

Jennifer looked even more confused. "But you *are* Cruiser, right?"

He would not answer that question because he wasn't sure who he was anymore. As she waited, her wet eyes looked him over as if taking a picture. Then she smiled and he thought he saw her lip quiver just a bit before she shook her head, then turned and walked up the beach and out of his life, all by herself and trying to be okay with that. A day would come for her to be as lonely as he was, and he *needed* that day to come for her. As disloyal as it made him feel, he hoped it came soon.

He stared at her tiny footprints in the sand and wished they were permanent and something of her he could keep. When he finally turned back toward the ocean he heard surfers whispering his name. He didn't look around as he pushed one arm through a shoulder strap of his wetsuit and pressed the Velcro together over the other shoulder.

He picked up his board and walked to the water. A dozen guys walked close by. He stopped at the water's edge to attach his leash, and when he did one teenager stepped out of the group. It was hard for Ernie to look at kids that age, knowing that Jennifer driving away meant he'd never have any kind of a family. God what an enormous price he'd paid.

"Excuse me, sir" the kid said, his head tilted against the rising sun and his hair hanging long on that side. "You're Ernie Roberts? For real? My dad says you're the surfer in the hurricane photo."

A lifetime of denying the truth tried to make him shrug it off as a mistake, but this was his first step toward a new life. "Yeah, I'm the guy," he said. "I'm the guy in the photo."

The kid turned toward his friends with a huge smile. He stood there like he was having his picture taken with a star.

Roberts looked back at the other surfers, who stared at him with the respect reserved for big wave riders. When the kid turned back, Roberts asked, "You going out?"

The kid looked at the surf. "Dunno. It's breaking clean, for sure, but there's no channel. Just one giant impact zone. Getting to the lineup is gonna be tough." He laughed nervously. "Might get killed just paddling out."

They stared together for a minute before the kid asked, "You going out?"

Roberts looked the kid over, then smiled and waded into the ocean until he was waist deep in water. He timed the waves of the killer shore break, and when he saw a chance he pushed his board ahead of him and slid onto it. He paddled like crazy through the foamy water, his hands digging fast toward the army of waves.

About the Author

Wes is a real-life adventurer, one of those people who turns life on its head and shakes the change from its pockets. A global traveler, yacht rat, intellectual, surf bum, bow-hunter, actor, romantic, former F.B.I./S.W.A.T. Agent and Security Consultant, raconteur and all-around fun guy, Wes can debate Voltaire and Rousseau while wrenching on a greasy diesel far out at sea, or drop into a point break wave as skillfully as he's crept within grasp of wild game.

Over the past dozen years Wes (wesdemott.com) has garnered international acclaim for his novels about prisoners of war, the FBI, military assassins, and spies. In his beautiful but heartbreaking novel, *Loving Zelda*, he wrote about hope and loss and the chance to change our lives if we're fearless enough to try.

Tortuga Gold reflects a fun new chapter in Wes's own life as he's joined in his adventures by his beautiful Belgian wife, Sabine, a human rights/refugee lawyer who spent seven of her fifteen years with the United Nations living in Africa, including full-time residency in the war zones of Rwanda, Burundi, and the Congo during their bloody genocides.

Wes's love of the ocean often plays into his short stories and novels. He's boated thousands of miles on dozens of his own boats, surfed world famous breaks, and caught or speared game fish since he was thirteen. In 2010, after sailing from the Chesapeake Bay to Florida's West Coast and selling their home, Wes and Sabine made a permanent move aboard their new boat, a trawler they named *Wasafiri* ("The Wanderers" in Swahili). After a shakedown cruise of 1200 miles, Wes took off for Bocas del Toro, Panama, planning to pick up Sabine in Isla Mujeres, Mexico. But the voyage was cut short when Wes shipwrecked in violent seas off the western tip of Cuba and was rescued by the Carnival Cruise ship, VALOR.

When Wes abandoned ship he left behind all their possessions except their cat and his American flag. Immediately after the Coast Guard told Sabine of the rescue, she texted a friend a message that well defines the way these two live: "Boat lost at sea. Wes and crew alive. All possessions gone. New adventures ahead."

The couple rented a flat in a Mexican beach town for a few months, and then, on June 1st, 2011, they moved to Portland, Oregon to begin exploring America's Pacific Northwest. Their shopping list of replacement items included backpacks, a good knife, Merrill hiking boots, and of course, another adventure hat for Wes.

There is really no way to guess where the couple will be by the time you read this.

NOVELS BY WES DEMOTT

THE TYPHOON SANCTION

CIA Field Officer Cruiser is a master at manipulating people and circumstances. Be careful or he'll manipulate you in this story of vengeance, murder, and global terrorism.

Mixing spies and counterespionage with old vendettas and small town murders, The Typhoon Sanction pits the protagonist, CIA Agent Jay Stewart, against a Chinese enemy who hunts him halfway around the world to the Outer Banks of North Carolina. Stewart's mastery of misdirection provides a whodunit element to this international thriller as the reader tries to make sense of four mysterious small-town murders. The more obvious the truth appears, the further the reader gets from it, ultimately being captured by the same skills that made Stewart such a successful operative.

THE FUND

How deep does the conspiracy go? Who's in charge and how many more will die? Aerospace engineer Peter Jamison is determined to find out.

While trying to save his contract for a tactical weapons system, Jamison uncovers a crime of corruption, power and violence that draws him into a deadly game he cannot win but still chooses to fight, any way he can.

This thriller has been translated into several languages and is an international best-seller and IPPY Gold Medal Award Recipient for Best Fiction. Robert Ludlum, the wonderfully gracious man that he was, hosted the launch party for this novel.

HEAT SYNC

Heat Sync takes you through the U.S. Assassination School exposed by NEWSWEEK Magazine just prior to this novel's publication.

Experience the pain and process of sanctioned murder from Lt. Henry Thompson, who was recruited for JASPERS from the U.S. Navy SEALS. Thompson believes he's training to assassinate foreign threats to this country, and it's only after he graduates and gets his orders that he realizes his true mission is to kill the President of the United States by using the White House access his girlfriend provides, and that he's already too boxed in by his handlers to refuse. Heat Sync provides an exciting but non-traditional thriller that deeply probes the emotions and psychology of a patriotic killer.

WALKING K

America's leaders haven't faced a Prisoner-of-War crisis since the debacle over POWs left behind in Vietnam. Walking K is an exciting thriller that exposes the reasons it can't be allowed to happen again.

DeMott, a former FBI Agent, analyzed intelligence documents, Nixon's White House tapes, Congressional Records, and interviewed POWs and their commanding officers while researching this tragic story of a reluctant conspiracy lumbered upon the shoulders of each U.S. President since 1975. Crosscutting between dramatic battlefield scenes, heartbreaking torture, American businesses protecting their investments, and a continuing refusal by the White House to reveal the shameful truth, the emotional ending of this thriller sadly shows why the United States Government stopped wanting the prisoners of that war to come home, and perhaps sheds light on the government's attitude toward the POW classification in wars since Vietnam.

LOVING ZELDA

The humanity and hope of this beautiful novel makes it the work for which Wes would most like to be remembered. Loving Zelda's emotional range includes pieces of everyone's past, and provides hope that we can all find love if we're brave enough to take a chance. Loving Zelda is an extremely rare glimpse of the soft-as-cotton heart of internationally known tough guy Wes DeMott.

Loving Zelda explores the emotional pain and damage inflicted on a writer's relationship with the woman he loves as she struggles with manic-depression. Through ten years of joy and hardship he loves and cares for her with unwavering devotion, but when she marries another man he becomes a recluse on his sailboat, waiting for a chance to be together again in this or any world.

TORTUGA GOLD

Throw your sea bag aboard WASAFIRI to join Taz Keaton and the Mayday Salvage and Rescue gang in fun adventures and a chance at Blackbeard's treasure.

Tortuga Gold is a fun action story that follows Taz's fast adventures after he rejects his wealthy lifestyle and starts Mayday Salvage and Rescue in search of excitement. After Taz and his two partners race the Panamanian National Police to recover a metal case from the wreckage of a private jet in a muddy river, they meet a man with a coin from an historic but never recovered Spanish shipment that vanished in 1715. From there the adventure rolls from modern day pirates to blood-sucking leeches, exploding yachts to beautiful international competitors and a sea battle with the legendary Blackbeard himself. This is the first novel in a series involving Taz and the Mayday crew.

COMING SOON

TEQUILA BOOM BOOM

After enjoying your thrill ride with Taz Keaton and the Mayday gang in TORTUGA GOLD, join them on another adventure in TEQUILA BOOM BOOM.

The Typhoon Sanction